Facing the Music

Bright Leaf Short Fiction VI   Shannon Ravenel, Series Editor

FACING TH

E MUSIC

STORIES

BY

Larry Brown

ALGONQUIN

BOOKS

OF

CHAPEL

HILL

1988

published by
Algonquin Books of Chapel Hill
Post Office Box 2225
Chapel Hill, North Carolina 27515-2225

in association with
Taylor Publishing Company
1550 West Mockingbird Lane
Dallas, Texas 75235

Several stories in this book have appeared
previously: "Boy and Dog" in *Fiction
International;* "Facing the Music" and
"The Rich" in *Mississippi Review;* "Kubuku
Rides (This Is It)" in *The Greensboro
Review;* "Samaritans" in *St. Andrews Review.*

Design by Molly Renda.

LIBRARY OF CONGRESS CATALOGING-IN-PUBLICATION DATA

Brown, Larry, 1951 July 9–
    Facing the music: stories / by Larry Brown.
    p. cm.—(Bright leaf short fiction: 6)

    Contents: Facing the music—Kubuku rides
(This is it)—The rich—Old Frank and Jesus—
Boy and dog—Julie—Samaritans—Night life
—Leaving town—The end of romance.

    ISBN 0-912697-91-1
    I. Title.   II. Series.

PS3552.R6927F3   1988
813'.54—dc 19   88-6304

FIRST EDITION

for Mary Annie

CONTENTS

Facing the Music

FACING THE MUSIC

For Richard Howorth

I cut my eyes sideways because I know what's coming. "You want the light off, honey?" she says. Very quietly.

I can see as well with it as without it. It's an old movie I'm watching, Ray Milland in *The Lost Weekend*. This character he's playing, this guy will do anything to get a drink. He'd sell children, probably, to get a drink. That's the kind of person Ray's playing.

Sometimes I have trouble resting at night, so I watch the movies until I get sleepy. They show them—all-night movies—on these stations from Memphis and Tupelo. There are probably a lot of people like me, unable to sleep, lying around watching them with me. I've got remote control so I can turn it on or off and change channels. She's stirring around the bedroom, doing things, doing something—I don't know what. She has to stay busy. Our children moved away and we don't have any pets.

We used to have a dog, a little brown one, but I accidentally killed it. Backed over its head with the station wagon one morning. She used to feed it in the kitchen, right after she came home from the hospital. But I told her, no more. It hurts too much to lose one.

"It doesn't matter," I say, finally, which is not what I'm thinking.

"That's Ray Milland," she says. "Wasn't he young then." Wistful like.

So he was. I was too once. So was she. So was everybody. But this movie is forty years old.

"You going to finish watching this?" she says. She sits on the bed right beside me. I'm propped up on the TV pillow. It's blue corduroy and I got it for Christmas last year. She said I was spending so much time in the bed, I might as well be comfortable. She also said it could be used for other things, too. I said what things?

I don't know why I have to be so mean to her, like it's her fault. She asks me if I want some more ice. I'm drinking whiskey. She knows it helps me. I'm not so much of a bastard that I don't know she loves me.

Actually, it's worse than that. I don't mean anything against God by saying this, but sometimes I think she worships me.

"I'm okay," I say. Ray has his booze hanging out the window on a string—hiding it from these booze-thieves he's trying to get away from—and before long he'll have to face the music. Ray can never find a good place to hide his booze. He gets so drunk he can't remember where he hid it when he sobers up.

Later on, he's going to try to write a novel, pecking the title and his name out with two fingers. But he's going to have a hard time. Ray is crazy about that booze, and doesn't even know how to type.

She may start rubbing on me. That's what I have to watch out for. That's what she does. She gets in bed with me when I'm watching a movie and she starts rubbing on me. I can't stand it. I especially can't stand for the light to be on when she does it. If the light's on when she does it, she winds up crying in the bathroom. That's the kind of husband I am.

But everything's okay, so far. She's not rubbing on me yet. I go ahead and mix myself another drink. I've got a whole bottle beside the bed. We had our Christmas party at the fire station the other night and everybody got a fifth. My wife didn't attend. She said every person in there would look at her. I told her they wouldn't, but I didn't argue much. I was on duty anyway and couldn't drink anything. All I could do was eat my steak and look around, go get another cup of coffee.

"I could do something for you," she says. She's teasing but she means it. I have to smile. One of those frozen ones. I feel like shooting both of us because she's fixed her hair up nice and she's got on a new nightgown.

"I could turn the lamp off," she says.

I have to be very careful. If I say the wrong thing, she'll take it the wrong way. She'll wind up crying in the bathroom if I say the wrong thing. I don't know what to say. Ray's just met this good-looking chick—Jane Wyman?—and I know he's going to steal a lady's purse later on; I don't want to miss it.

I could do the things Ray Milland is doing in this movie and worse. Boy. Could I. But she's right over here beside my face wanting an answer. Now. She's smiling at me. She's licking her lips. I don't want to give in. Giving in leads to other things, other givings.

I have to say something. But I don't say anything.

She gets up and goes back over to her dressing table. She picks up her brush. I can hear her raking and tearing it through her hair. It sounds like she's ripping it out by the roots. I have to stay here and listen to it. I can understand why people jump off bridges.

"You want a drink?" I say. "I can mix you up a little bourbon and Coke."

"I've got some," she says, and she lifts her can to show me. Diet Coke. At least a six-pack a day. The refrigerator's crammed full of them. I can hardly get to my beer for them. I think they're only one calorie or something. She thinks she's fat and that's the reason I don't pay enough attention to her, but it isn't.

She's been hurt. I know she has. You can lie around the house all your life and think you're safe. But you're not. Something from outside or inside can reach out and get you. You can get sick and have to go to the hospital. Some nut could walk into the station one night and kill us all in our beds. You can read about things like that in the paper any morning you want to. I try not to think about it. I just do my job and then come home and try to stay in the house with her. But sometimes I can't.

Last week, I was in this bar in town. I'd gone down there with some of these boys we're breaking in, rookies. Just young boys, nineteen or twenty. They'd passed probation and wanted to celebrate, so a few of us older guys went with them. We drank a few pitchers and listened to the band. It was a pretty good band. They did a lot of Willie and Waylon stuff. I'm thinking about all this while she's getting up and moving around the room, looking out the windows.

I don't go looking for things—I don't—but later on, well, there was this woman in there. Not a young woman. Younger than me. About forty. She was sitting by herself. I was in no hurry to go home. All the boys had gone, Bradshaw, too. I was the only one of the group left. So I said what the hell. I went up to the bar and bought two drinks and carried them over to her table. I sat down with them and I smiled at her. And she smiled back. In an hour we were over at her house.

I don't know why I did it. I'd never done anything like that before. She had some money. You could tell it from her house and things. I was a little drunk, but I know that's no excuse. She took me into her bedroom and she put a record on, some nice slow orchestra or something. I was lying on the bed the whole time, knowing my wife was at home waiting up on me. This woman stood up in the middle of the room and started turning. She had her arms over her head. She had white hair piled up high. When she took off her jacket, I could tell she had something nice underneath. She took off her shirt, and her breasts were like something you'd see in a movie, deep long things you might only glimpse in a swimming suit. Before I knew it, she was on the bed with me, putting one of them in my mouth.

"You sure you don't want a drink?" I say.

"I want you," she says, and I don't know what to say. She's not looking at me. She's looking out the window. Ray's coming out of the bathroom now with the lady's purse under his arm. But I know they're all going to be waiting for him, the whole club. I know what he's going to feel. Everybody's going to be looking at him.

When this woman got on top of me, the only thing I could think was: God.

"What are we going to do?" my wife says.

"Nothing," I say. But I don't know what I'm saying. I've got these big soft nipples in my mouth and I can't think of anything else. I'm trying to remember exactly how it was.

I thought I'd be different somehow, changed. I thought she'd know what I'd done just by looking at me. But she didn't. She didn't even notice.

I look at her and her shoulders are jerking under the little green gown. I'm always making her cry and I don't mean to. Here's the kind of bastard I am: my wife's crying because she wants me, and I'm lying here watching Ray Milland, and drinking whiskey, and thinking about putting another woman's breasts in my mouth. She was on top of me and they were hanging right over my face. It was so wonderful, but now it seems so awful I can hardly stand to think about it.

"I understand how you feel," she says. "But how do you think I feel?"

She's not talking to me; she's talking to the window and Ray is staggering down the street in the hot sunshine, looking for a pawnshop so he can hock the typewriter he was going to use to write his novel.

A commercial comes on, a man selling dog food. I can't just sit here and not say anything. I have to say something. But, God, it hurts to.

"I know," I say. It's almost the same as saying nothing. It doesn't mean anything.

We've been married for twenty-three years.

"You don't know," she says. "You don't know the things that go through my mind."

I know what she's going to say. I know the things going through her mind. She's seeing me on top of her with her legs over my shoulders, her legs locked around my back. But she won't take her gown off anymore. She'll just push it up. She never takes her gown off, doesn't want me to see. I know what will happen. I can't do anything about it. Before long she'll be over here rubbing on me, and if I don't start, she'll stop and wind up crying in the bathroom.

"Why don't you have a drink?" I say. I wish she'd have a drink. Or go to sleep. Or just watch the movie with me. Why can't she just watch the movie with me?

"I should have just died," she says. "Then you could have gotten you somebody else."

I guess maybe she means somebody like the friendly woman with the nice house and the nice nipples.

I don't know. I can't find a comfortable place for my neck.

"You shouldn't say that."

"Well it's true. I'm not a whole woman anymore. I'm just a burden on you."

"You're not."

"Well you don't want me since the operation."

She's always saying that. She wants me to admit it. And I don't want to lie anymore, I don't want to spare her feelings anymore, I want her to know I've got feelings too and it's hurt me almost as bad as it has her. But that's not what I say. I can't say that.

"I do want you," I say. I have to say it. She makes me say it.

"Then prove it," she says. She comes close to the bed and she leans over me. She's painted her brows with black stuff and her face is made up to where I can hardly believe it.

"You've got too much makeup on," I whisper.

She leaves. She's in the bathroom scrubbing. I can hear the water running. Ray's got the blind staggers. Everybody's hiding his whiskey from him and he can't get a drink. He's got it bad. He's on his way to the nuthouse.

Don't feel like a lone ranger, Ray.

The water stops running. She cuts the light off in there and then she steps out. I don't look around. I'm watching a hardware store commercial. Hammers and Skilsaws are on the wall. They always have this pretty girl with large breasts selling their hardware. The big special this week is garden hose. You can buy a hundred feet, she says, for less than four dollars.

The TV is just a dim gray spot between my socks. She's getting on the bed, setting one knee down and pulling up the hem of her gown. She can't wait. I'm thinking of it again, how the woman's breasts looked, how she looked in her shirt before she took it off, how I could tell she had something nice underneath, and how wonderful it was to be drunk in that moment when I knew what she was going to do.

It's time now. She's touching me. Her hands are moving, sliding all over me. Everywhere. Ray is typing with two fingers somewhere, just the title and his name. I can hear the pecking of his keys. That old boy, he's trying to do what he knows he should. He has responsibilities to people who love him and need him; he can't let them down. But he's scared to death. He doesn't know where to start.

"You going to keep watching this?" she says, but dreamy-like, kissing me, as if she doesn't care one way or the other.

I don't say anything when I cut the TV off. I can't speak. I'm thinking of how it was on our honeymoon, in that little room at Hattiesburg, when she bent her arms behind her back and slumped her shoulders forward, how the cups loosened and fell as the straps slid off her arms. I'm thinking that your first love is your best love, that you'll never find any better. The way she did it was like she was saying, here I am, I'm all yours, all of me, forever. Nothing's changed. She turns the light off, and we reach to find each other in the darkness like people who are blind.

KUBUKU RIDES

(This Is It)

Angel hear the back door slam. It Alan, in from work. She start to hide the glass and then she don't hide the glass, he got a nose like a bloodhound and gonna smell it anyway, so she just keep sitting on the couch. She gonna act like nothing happening, like everything cool. Little boy in the yard playing, he don't know nothing. He think Mama in here watching Andy Griffith. Cooking supper. She better now anyway. Just wine, beer, no whiskey, no vodka. No gin. She getting well, she gonna make it. He have to be patient with her. She trying. He no rose garden himself anyway.

She start to get up and then she don't, it better if she stay down like nothing going on. She nervous, though. She know he looking, trying to catch her messing up. He watch her like a hawk, like somebody with eyes in the back of they head. He don't miss much. He come into the room and he see her. She

11

smile, try to, but it wrong, she know it wrong, she guilty. He
see it. He been out loading lumber or something all day long,
he tired and ready for supper. But ain't no supper yet. She know
all this and ain't said nothing. She scared to speak because she
so guilty. But she mad over having to *feel* guilty, because some
of this guilt *his* fault. Not all his fault. But some of it. Maybe
half. Maybe less. This thing been going on a while. This thing
nothing new.

"Hey honey," she say.

"I done unloaded two tons of two-by-fours today," he say.

"You poor baby," she say. "Come on and have a little drink
with Mama." That the wrong thing to say.

"What?" he say. "You drinkin again? I done told you and
told you and told you."

"It's just wine," she say.

"Well woman how many you done had?"

"This just my first one," she say, but she lying. She done
had five and ain't even took nothing out the deep freeze. Wind
up having a turkey pot pie or something. Something don't nobody want. She can't cook while she trying to figure out what
to do. Don't know what to do. Ain't gonna drink nothing at all
when she get up. Worries all day about drinking, then in the
evening she done worried so much over *not* drinking she starts
in drinking. She in one of them vicious circles. She done even
thought about doing away with herself, but she hate to leave her
husband and her little boy alone in the world. Probably mess
her little boy up for the rest of his life. She don't want to die
anyway. Angel ain't but about thirty years old. She still good-

looking, too. And love her husband like God love Jesus. Ain't no answer, that's it.

"Where that bottle?" he say.

Now she gonna act like she don't know what he talking about. "What bottle?" she say.

"Hell, woman. Bottle you drinkin from. What you mean what bottle?"

She scared now, frightened of his wrath. He don't usually go off. But he go off on her drinking in a minute. He put up with anything but her drinking.

"It's in the fridge," she say.

He run in there. She hear him open the door. He going to bust it in a million pieces. She get up and go after him, wobbly. She grabbing for doors and stuff, trying to get in there. He done took her money away, she can't have no more. He don't let her write no checks. He holding the bottle up where she can see it good. The contents of that bottle done trashed.

He say, "First glass my ass."

"Oh, Alan," she say. "That a old bottle."

"Old bottle? That what you say, old bottle?"

"I found it," she say.

"Lyin!" he say.

She shake her head no no no no no. She wanting that last drink because everything else hid.

"What you mean goin out buying some more?" he say. He got veins standing up in his neck. He mad, he madder than she ever seen him.

"Oh, Alan, please," she say. She hate herself begging like

this. She ready to get down on her knees if she have to, though.

"I found it," she say.

"You been to the liquor store. Come on, now," he say. "You been to the liquor store, ain't you?"

Angel start to say something, start to scream something, but she see Randy come in from the front yard. He stop behind his daddy. Mama fixing to get down in the floor for that bottle. Daddy yelling stuff. Ain't no good time to come in. He eight year old but he know what going on. He tiptoe back out.

"Don't pour it out," she say. "Just let me finish it and I'll quit. Start supper," she say.

"Lie to me," he say. "Lie to me and take money and promise. How many times you promised?"

She go to him. He put the bottle behind his back, saying, "Don't, now, baby." He moaning, like.

"Alan *please,*" she say. She put one arm around his waist and try for that bottle. He stronger than her. It ain't fair! They stumble around in the kitchen. She trying for the bottle, he heading for the sink, she trying to get it. Done done this before. Ain't no fun no more.

He say, "I done told you what I'm goin to do."

She say, "Just let me finish it, Alan. Don't make me beg," she say. Ain't no way she hold him, he too strong. Lift weights three days a week. Runs. Got muscles like concrete. Know how to box but don't never hit her. She done hit him plenty with her little drunk fists, ain't hurt him, though. He turn away and start taking the cap off the bottle. She grab for it. She got both hands on it. He trying to pull it away. She panting. He pulling the bottle away, down in the sink so he can pour it out. They going to break it. Somebody going to get cut. May be him, may be her. Don't matter who. They tugging, back and forth, up and down. Ain't nobody in they right mind.

"Let go!" she say. She know Randy hearing it. He done run away once. Ain't enough for her. Ought to be but ain't.

He jerk it away and it hit the side of the sink and break. Blood gushing out of his hand. Mixing with the wine. Blood and wine all over the sink. Don't look good. Look bad. Look like maybe somebody have to kill theirself before it all get over with. Can't keep on like this. Done gone on too long.

"Godomightydamn," he say. Done sliced his hand wide open. It bad, she don't know how bad. Angel don't want to see. She run back to the living room for the rest of that glass. She don't drink it, he'll get it. She grab it. Pour it down. Two inches of wine. Then it all gone. She throw the glass into the mirror and everything break. Alan yell something in the kitchen and she run back in there and look. He got a bloody towel wrap around his hand. Done unloaded two tons of wood today and hospital bill gonna be more than he made. Won't take fifteen minutes. Emergency room robbery take longer than plain robbery but don't require no gun.

He shout, "This is it!" He crying and he don't cry. "Can't stand it! Sick of it!"

She sick too. He won't leave her alone. He love her. He done cut his hand wide open because of this love. He crying, little boy terrified. He run off again, somebody liable to snatch him up and they never see him again. Ought to be enough but ain't. Ain't never enough.

She flashing back now. She done had a wreck a few weeks ago. She done went out with some friends of hern, Betty and Glynnis and Sue. She done bought clothes for Randy and towels for her mama and cowboy boots for Alan. Pretty ones. Rhino's hide and hippo's toes. She working then, she still have a job then. It a Saturday. Randy and Alan at Randy's Little League game. She think she going over later, but she never make it. She get drunk instead.

They gone have just one little drink, her and Betty and Sue and them. One little drink ain't gone hurt nothing or nobody. Betty telling about her divorce and new men she checking out. She don't give no details, though. They drinking a light white wine but Angel having a double One Fifty-One and Coke. She ain't messing around. This a few weeks ago, she ain't got time for no wine. And she drink hers off real quick and order and get another one before they even get they wines down. She think maybe they won't even notice she done had two, they all so busy listening to Betty telling about these wimps she messing with. But it ain't even interesting and they notice right away. Angel going to the game, though. She definitely going to the game. She done promised everybody in the country. Time done come where she have to be straight. She got to quit breaking these promises. She got to quit all this lying and conniving.

Then before long they start talking about leaving. She ask them to stay, say Please, ya'll just stay and have one more. But naw, they got to go. Glynnis, she claim she got this hot date tonight. She talk like she got a hot date every night. Betty got this new man she going out with and she got to roll her hair and stuff. But Sue now is true. Angel done went to high school with her. They was in school together back when they was wearing hot pants and stuff. This like a old relationship. But Sue know what going on. She just hate to say anything. She just hate to bring it out in the wide open. She got to say something, though. She wait till the rest of them go and then she speak up.

She say, "I thought you goin to the ball game, girl." She look at her watch.

"Yeah," Angel say. "Honey, I'm goin. I wouldn't miss it for the world. But first I got to have me some more One Fifty-One and Coke."

Sue know she lying. She done lied to everybody about everything. This thing a problem can't keep quiet. She done had troubles at work. She done called in late, and sick, done called in and lied like a dog about her physical condition with these hungovers.

Now Angel hurting. She know Sue know the truth but too good to nag. She know Sue one good person she can depend on the rest of her life, but she know too Sue ain't putting up with her killing herself in her midst. She know Sue gone say something, but Sue don't say nothing until she finish her second wine. This after Angel ask her to have a third wine. Somebody got to stop her. She keep on, she be asking to stay for a eighth and a ninth wine. She be asking to stay till the place close down.

So Sue say, "You gone miss that ball game, girl."

She say she already late. She motion for another drink. Sue reach over and put her hand over Angel's glass and say, "Don't do that, girl."

"Late already," she say. "One more won't make no difference."

She know her speech and stuff messed up. It embarrassing, but the barmaid, she bring the drink. And Sue reach out, put her hand over the glass and say, "Don't you give her that shit, woman."

Girl back up and say, "*Ma'am?*" Real nice like.

"Don't you give her that," say Sue.

Girl say, "Yes'm, but ma'am, she order it, ma'am."

Girl look at Angel.

"Thank you, hon," she say. She reach and take the drink and give the girl some money. Then she tip her a dollar and the girl walk away. Angel grab this drink and slosh some of it out on her. She know it but she can't help it. She don't know what went wrong. She shopping and going to the ball game and now this done happened again. She ain't making no ball game. Ball game done shot to hell. She be in perhaps two three in the morning.

Sue now, she tired of this.

"When you goin to admit it?" she say.

"Admit what?"

"Girl, *you* know. Layin drunk. Runnin around here drinkin every night. Stayin out."

She say, "I don't know what you talkin about," like she huffy. She drinking every day. Even Sunday. Especially Sunday. Sunday the worst because ain't nothing open. She don't hit the liquor store Saturday night she climbing the walls Sunday afternoon. She done even got drunk and listened to the services on TV Sunday morning and got all depressed and passed out before dinnertime. Then Alan and Randy have to eat them turkey pot pies again.

"Alan and Randy don't understand me," she say.

"They love you," Sue say.

"And I love them," she say.

"Listen now," Sue tell her, "you gonna lose that baby and that man if you don't stop this messin around."

"Ain't gonna do that no such of a thing," she say, but she know Sue right. She still pouring that rum down, she ain't slacked off. She just have to deny the truth because old truth hurt too much to face.

Sue get up, she got tears in her eye and stuff, she dabbing with Kleenexes. Can't nobody talk sense to this fool.

"Yes you will," she say, and she leave. She ain't gone hang around and watch this self-destruction. Woman done turned into a time bomb ticking. She got to get away from here, so she run out the door. She booking home. Everybody looking.

Angel all alone now. She order two more singles and drink both of them. But she shitfaced time she drink that last one, she done been in the booth a hour and a half. Which has done caused some men to think about hitting on her, they done seen them thin legs and stuff she got. This one wimp done even come over to the table, he just assume she lonesome and want some male company, he think he gonna come over like he Robert Goulet or somebody and just invite himself to sit down. He done seen her wedding ring, but he thinking, Man, this woman horny or something, she wouldn't be sitting here all by her lonesome. And this fool almost sit down in the booth with her, he gonna buy her a drink, talk some trash to her, when he really thinking is he gonna get her in some motel room and take her panties off. But she done recognized his act, she ain't having nothing to do with this fool. She tell him off right quick. Of course he get huffy and leave. That's fine. Ain't asked that fool to sit down with her anyway.

Now she done decided she don't want to have another drink in this place. Old depression setting in. People coming in now to eat seafood with they families, little kids and stuff, grand-mamas, she don't need to be hanging around in here no more. Waiters looking at her. She know they wanting her to leave before she give their place a bad name. Plus she taking up room in this booth where some family wanting to eat some filet catfish. She know all this stuff. She know she better leave before they ask her to. She done had embarrassment enough, don't need no more.

Ain't eat nothing yet. Don't want nothing to eat. Don't even eat at home much. Done lost weight, breasts done come down, was fine and full, legs even done got skinny. She know Alan notice it when she undress. She don't even weigh what she weigh on they wedding night when she give herself to Alan. She know he worried sick about her. He get her in the bed and squeeze her so tight he hurt her, but she don't say Let go.

She trying to walk straight when she go out to her car, but she look like somebody afflicted. Bumping into hoods and stuff. She done late already. Ball game over. It after six and Randy and Alan already home by now. Ain't no way she going home right now. She ain't gonna face them crying faces. And, too, she go home, Alan ain't letting her drink another drop. So she decide to get her a bottle and just ride around a while. She gonna ride around and sober up, then she gonna go home. And she need to do this anyway because this give her time to think something up like say the car tore up or something, why she late.

Only thing, she done gone in the liquor store so many times she ashamed to. She see these same people and she know they thinking: Damn, this woman done been in here four times this week. Drinking like a fish. She don't like to look in they eyes. So she hunt her up another store on the other side of town. She don't want to get too drunk, so she just get a sixer of beers and some schnapps. She going to ride around, cruise a little and sober up. That what she thinking.

She driving okay. Hitting them beers occasionally, hitting that peach schnapps every few minutes because it so good and ain't but forty-eight proof. It so weak it ain't gonna make her drunk. Not no half pint. She ain't gonna ride around but a hour. Then she gonna go home.

She afraid to take a drink when anybody behind her. She

thinking the police gonna see her and throw them blue lights on her. Then she be in jail calling Alan to come bail her out. Which he already done twice before. She don't want to stay in town. She gonna drive out on the lake road. They not as much traffic out there. So she go off out there, on this blacktop road. She gonna ride out to the boat landing. Ain't nobody out there, it too cold to fish. She curve around through the woods three or four miles. She done finished one of them beers and throwed the bottle out the window. She get her another one and drink some more of that schnapps. That stuff go down so easy and so hard to stop on. Usually when she open a half pint, she throw the cap far as she can.

Angel weaving a little, but she ain't drunk. She just a little tired. She wishing she home in the bed right now. She know they gonna have a big argument when she get home. She dreading that. Alan, he have to fix supper for Randy and his mama ain't taught him nothing about cooking. Only thing he know how to do is warm up a TV dinner, and Randy just sull up when he have to eat one of them. She wishing now she'd just gone on home. Wouldn't have been so bad then. Going to be worse now, much worser than if she'd just gone on home after them double One Fifty-Ones. Way it is, though. Get started, can't stop. Take that first drink, she ain't gonna stop till she pass out or run out. She don't know what it is. She ain't even understand it herself. Didn't start out like this. Didn't use to be this way. Use to be a beer once in a while, little wine at New Year's. Things just get out of hand. Don't mean to be this way. Just can't help it. Alan used to would drink a little beer on weekends and it done turned him flat against it. He don't even want to be around nobody drinking now. Somebody offer him a drink now he tell em to get it out of his face. He done even lost some of his friends over this thing.

Angel get down to the boat ramp, ain't a soul there. Windy out there, water dark, scare her to death just to see it. What would it be to be out in them waves, them black waves closing over your head, ain't nobody around to hear you screaming. Coat be waterlogged and pulling you down. Hurt just a little and that's all. Just a brief pain. Be dead then, won't know nothing. Won't have no hurts. Easy way out. They get over it eventually. Could make it look like an accident. Drive her car right off in the water, everybody think it a mistake. Just a tragedy, that's all, a unfortunate thing. Don't want to hurt nobody. What so wrong with her life she do the things she do? Killing her baby and her man little at a time. And her ownself. But have to have it. Thinking things when she drinking she wouldn't think at all when she not drinking. But now she drinking all the time, and she thinking same way all the time.

She drink some more beer and schnapps, and then she pass out or go to sleep, she don't know which. Same thing. Sleeping she don't have to think no more. Ain't no hurting when she sleeping. Sleeping good, but can't sleep forever. Somebody done woke her up, knocking on the glass. Some boy out there. High school boy. Truck parked beside, some more kids in it. She scared at first, think something bad. But they look all right.

Don't look mean or nothing. Just look worried. She get up and roll her window down just a little, just crack it.

"Ma'am?" this boy say. "You all right, ma'am?"

"Yes," she say. "Fine, thank you."

"Seen you settin here," he say. "Thought your car tore up maybe."

"No," Angel say. "Just sleepy," she say. "Leavin now," she say, and she roll the window up. She turn the lights on, car still running, ain't even shut it off. Out in the middle of nowhere asleep, ain't locked the door. Somebody walk up and slit her throat, she not even know it. She crazy. She got to get home. She done been asleep no telling how long.

She afraid they gonna follow her out. They do. She can't stand for nobody to get behind her like that. Make her nervous. She decide she gonna speed up and leave them behind. She get up to about sixty-five. She start to pull away. She sobered up a little while she asleep. Be okay to get another one of them beers out the sack now. Beer sack down in the floor. Have to lean over and take her eyes off the road just a second to get that beer, no problem.

Her face hit the windshield, the seat slam her up. Too quick. Lights shining up against a tree. Don't even know what happened. Windshield broke all to pieces. Smoke coming out the hood. She wiping her face. Interior light on, she got blood all over her hands. Face bleeding. She look in the rearview mirror, she don't know her own self. Look like something in a monster movie. She screaming now. Face cut all to pieces. She black out again. She come to, she out on the ground. People helping her up. She screaming I'm ruint I'm ruint. Lights in her eyes, legs moving in front of her. Kids talking. One of them say she just drive right off the road into that tree. She don't believe it. Road move or something. Tree jump out in front of her. She a good driver. She drive too good for something like this.

Cost three thousand dollars to fix the car this time. Don't even drive right no more. Alan say the frame bent. Alan say it won't never drive right no more. And ain't even paid for. She don't know about no frame. She just know it jerk going down the road.

She in the hospital a while. She don't remember exactly, three or four days. They done had to sew her face up. People see them scars even through thick makeup the rest of her life. She bruised so bad she don't get out the bed for a week. Alan keep saying they lucky she ain't dead. He keep praising God his wife ain't dead. She know she just gonna have to go through it again now sometime, till a worse one happen. Police done come and talked to her. She lie her way out of it, though. Can't prove nothing. Alan keep saying we lucky.

Ain't lucky. Boss call, want to know when she coming back to work. She hem and haw. Done missed all them Mondays. She can't give no definite answer. He clear his throat. Maybe he should find somebody else for her position since she so vague. Well yessir, she say, yessir, if you think that the best thing.

Alan awful quiet after this happen. He just sit and stare. She touch him out on the porch, he just draw away. Like her hand a bad thing to feel on him. This go on about a week. Then he come home from work one evening and she sitting in the living room with a glass of wine in her hand.

He back now from having his hand sewed up. He sitting in the kitchen drinking coffee, he done bought some cigarettes and he smoking one after another. Done been quit two years, say it the hardest thing he ever done. He say he never stop wanting one, that he have to brace himself every day. Now he done started back. She know: This what she done to him.

Angel not drinking anything. Don't mean she don't have nothing. Just can't have it right now. He awake now. Later he be asleep. He think the house clean. House ain't clean. Lots of places to hide things, you want to hide them bad enough. Ain't like Easter eggs, like Christmas presents. Like life and death.

Wouldn't never think on her wedding night it ever be like this. She in the living room by herself, he in the kitchen by himself. TV on, she ain't watching it, some fool on Johnny Carson telling stuff ain't even funny. She ain't got the sound on. Ain't hear nothing, ain't see nothing. She hear him like choke in there once in a while. Randy in the bed asleep. Want so bad to get up and go in there and tell Alan, Baby I promise I will quit. Again. But ain't no use in saying it, she don't mean it. Just words. Don't mean nothing. Done lost trust anyway. Lose trust, a man and wife, done lost everything. Even if she quit now, stay quit, he always be looking over that shoulder, he always be smelling her breath. Lost his trust she won't never get it back.

He come in there where she at finally. He been crying, she

tell it by looking at him. He not hurting for himself, he not hurting for his hand. He cut off his hand and throw it away she ask him to. He hurting for her. She know all this, don't nobody have to tell her. Why it don't do no good to talk to her. She know it all already.

"Baby," he say. "I goin to bed. Had a long day today."

His face look like he about sixty years old. He thirty-one. Weigh one sixty-five and bench press two-ninety. "You comin?" he say.

She want to. Morning be soon enough to drink something else. He be gone to work, Randy be gone to school. House be quiet by seven-thirty. She do what she want to then. Whole day be hers to do what she want to. Things be better tomorrow maybe. She cook them something good for supper, she make them a good old pie and have ice cream. She get better. They know she trying. She just weak, she just need some time. This thing not something you throw off like a cold. This thing deep, this thing beat more good people than her.

Angel say, "Not just yet, baby. I going to sit in here in the livin room a while. I so sorry you cut your hand," she say.

"You want to move?" he say. "Another state? Another country? You say the word I quit my job tomorrow. Don't matter. Just a job," he say.

"Don't want to move," she say. She trembling.

"Don't matter what people thinks," he say.

She think he gonna come over and get down on the floor and hug her knees and cry, but he don't. He look like he holding back to keep from doing that. And she glad he don't. He do that, she make them promises again. She promise anything if he just stop.

"Okay," he say. "I goin to bed now." He look beat.

He go. She by herself. It real quiet now. Hear anything. Hear walls pop, hear mice move. They eating something in the cabinet, she need to set some traps.

Time go by so slow. She know he in there listening. He listen for any step she make, which room she move into, which furniture she reach for. She have to wait. It risky now. He think she in here drinking, they gonna have it all over again. One time a night enough. Smart thing is go to bed. Get next to him. That what he want. Ought to be what she want. Use to be she did.

Thirty minutes a long time like this. She holding her breath when she go in there to look at him. He just a lump in the dark. Can't tell if he sleeping or not. Could be laying there looking at her. Too dark to tell. He probably asleep, though. He tired, he give out. He work so hard for them.

Tomorrow be better. Tomorrow she have to try harder. She know she can do it, she got will power. Just need a little time. They have to be patient with her. Ain't built Rome in a day. And she gonna be so good in the future, it ain't gonna hurt nothing to have a few cold beers tonight. Ain't drinking no whiskey now. Liquor store done closed anyway. Big Star still open. She just run down get some beer and then run right back. Don't need to drink what she got hid anyway. Probably won't need none later, she gonna quit anyway, but just in case.

She know where the checkbook laying. She ain't making

no noise. If he awake he ain't saying nothing. If he awake he'd be done said something. He won't know she ever been gone. Won't miss no three dollar check no way. Put it in with groceries sometime.

Side door squeak every time. Don't never notice it in daytime. Squeak like hell at night. Porch light on. He always leave it on if she going to be out. Ain't no need to turn it off. She be back in ten minutes. He never know she gone. Car in the driveway. It raining. A little.

Ain't cold. Don't need no coat.

She get in, ease the door to. Trying to be quiet. He so tired, he need his rest. She look at the bedroom window when she turn the key. And the light come on in there.

Caught now. Wasn't even asleep. Trying to just catch her on purpose. Laying in there in the dark just making out like he asleep. Don't trust her. Won't never trust her. It like he making her slip around. Damn him anyway.

Ain't nothing to do but talk to him. He standing on the step in his underwear. She put it in reverse and back on up. She stop beside him and roll down the window. She hate to. Neighbors gonna see him out here in his underwear. What he think he doing anyway, can't leave her alone. Treat her like some baby he can't take his eye off of for five minutes.

"I just goin to the store," she say. "I be right back."

"Don't care for you goin to the store," he say. "Long as you come back. You comin back?"

He got his arms wrapped around him, he shivering in the night air. He look like he been asleep.

"I just goin after some cigarettes," she say. "I be back in ten minutes. Go on back to bed. I be right back. I promise."

He step off the porch and come next the car. He hugging himself and shaking, barefooted. Standing in the driveway getting wet.

"I won't say nothin about you drinkin if you just do it at home," he say. "Go git you somethin to drink. But come back home," he say. "Please," he say.

It hit her now, this enough. This enough to stop anything, anybody, everything. He done give up.

"Baby," he say, "know you ain't gone stop. Done said all I can say. Just don't get out on the road drinkin. Don't care about the car. Just don't hurt yourself."

"I done told you I be back in ten minutes," she say. "I be *back* in ten minutes."

Something cross his face. Can't tell rain from tears in this. But what he shivering from she don't think is cold.

"Okay, baby," he say, "okay," and he turn away. She relieved. Now maybe won't be no argument. Now maybe won't be no dread. She telling the truth anyway. Ain't going nowhere but Big Star. Be back in ten minutes. All this fussing for nothing. Neighbors probably looking out the windows.

He go up on the porch and put his hand on the door. He watching her back out the driveway, she watching him standing there half naked. All this foolishness over a little trip to Big Star. She shake her head while she backing out the driveway. It almost like he ain't even expecting her to come back. She almost laugh at this. Ain't nothing even open this late but bars, and she *ain't* going to none of them, no ma'am. She see him watch her again, and then she see him step inside. What he need to do. Go on back to bed, get him some rest. He got to go to work in the morning. All she got to do is sleep.

She turn the wipers on to see better. The porch light shining out there, yellow light showing rain, it slanting down hard. It shine on the driveway and on Randy's bicycle and on they barbecue grill setting there getting wet. It make her feel good to know this all hers, that she always got this to come back to. This light show her home, this warm place she own that mean everything to her. This light, it always on for her. That what she thinking when it go out.

THE RICH

Mr. Pellisher works at the travel agency, and he associates with the rich. Sometimes the rich stop by in the afternoon hours when the working citizens have fled the streets to punch their clocks. The rich are strangers to TUE IN 6:57 OUT 12:01 IN 12:29 OUT 3:30. Mr. Pellisher keeps his punch clock carefully hidden behind stacks of travel folders, as if he's on straight salary. As if he's like the rich, free of the earthly shackles of timekeepers. He keeps a pot of coffee on hot for the rich, in case the rich deign to share a cup with him, even though Mr. Pellisher pays for the coffee himself.

But the rich don't drink coffee in the afternoons. The rich favor Campari and soda, Perrier, and old, old bottles of wine. The rich are impertinent. The rich are impatient. The rich are rich.

Mr. Pellisher can see the rich coming from his office window, where he pores over folders of sunny beaches and waving palms, of cliff divers and oyster divers. The rich arrive in Lincolns white and shimmering, hubcaps glittering like diamonds. They are long and sleek, these cars the rich drive, and clean. No one has ever puked on the floormats of a car belonging to the rich. Empty potato chip bags and candy wrappers are not to be found—along with Coke cans and plastic straws—on the car seats of the rich. If they are, they were dropped there by the rich.

He straightens his tie when he sees the rich coming, and sets out styrofoam cups and sugar cubes. He straightens his desk and pulls out chairs, waiting for the rich. And when the rich push the door open, he springs from his desk, hand offered in offertory handshake. But the handshakes of the rich are limp, without feeling, devoid of emotion. Mr. Pellisher pumps the hands of the rich as if he'd milk the money from their fingers. The fingers of the rich are fat and white, like overgrown grubs. Mr. Pellisher offers the rich a seat. He offers coffee. The rich decline both with one fat wave of their puffy white hands. The rich often wear gold chains around their necks. Most of the rich wear diamond rings. Some of the rich wear gold bones in their noses. A lot of the rich, especially the older rich, have been surgically renovated. The rich can afford tucks and snips. With their rich clothes off, most of the rich are all wrinkles below their chins.

The rich live too richly. The rich are pampered. The rich are spoiled by the poor, who want to be rich. To Mr. Pellisher, who is poor, the rich are symbols to look up to, standards of excellence which must be strived for. The rich, for instance, are always taking vacations.

Mr. Pellisher turns the air-conditioning up a notch in his office, as the rich begin to sweat. He offers coffee again. The rich refuse. The rich have only two minutes to spare. They must lay their plans in the capable hands of Mr. Pellisher and depart to whatever richening schemes the rich pursue. Just one time Mr. Pellisher would like to take a vacation like the rich do, and see the things the rich see, and have sex with the women the rich have sex with. He often wonders about the sex lives of the rich. He speculates upon how the rich procure women. Do the rich advertise? Do the rich seek out the haunts of other rich, in the hope of ferreting out rich nymphomaniacs? Or do the rich hire people to arrange their sex? Just how do the rich make small talk in bars where only strangers abound? Do the rich say, "I'm rich," and let it go at that? Or do the rich glide skillfully into a conversation with talk of stocks and bonds? Are the rich perverted? Do the rich perform unnatural sex acts? Can the rich ever be horny? Do the rich have sex every night? Watch kung-fu quickies? Eat TV dinners? Buy their own beer? Wash their own dishes? Are the rich so different from himself?

He thinks they are not. He knows they are only rich. And if some way, somehow, he could be rich, too, he knows he would be exactly like them. He knows he would be invited to their parties. Summoned to their art exhibits. Called from the dark confines of his own huge monstrous cool castle to sit at the tables of other rich and tell witty anecdotes, of which he has many in great supply. He knows the rich are not different from himself. They are not of another race, another creed, another skin. They do not worship a different God.

Mr. Pellisher has many travel folders. He spreads them before the rich, as a man would fan a deck of cards. He has all the points of the globe at his fingertips, like the rich, and he can make arrangements through a small tan telephone that sits on his desk. He is urgent, ready. He has a Xeroxed copy of international numbers taped beneath the Plexiglas that covers his desk. He can send the rich to any remote or unremote corner of the world with expert flicks of his fingers. He can line up hotels, vistas, visas, Visacards, passports, make reservations, secure hunting licenses, hire guides, Sherpas, serfs, peasants, waiters, cocktail waitresses, gardeners, veterinarians, prostitutes, bookies, make bets, cover point-spreads, confirm weather conditions, reserve yachts, captains, second mates, rods, reels, secure theater tickets, perform transactions, check hostile environments in third-world countries, wire money, locate cocaine, buy condos, close down factories, watch the stock market, buy, sell, trade, steal. With his phone, with the blessing of the rich, he is as the rich. He is their servant, their confidant, their messenger. He is everything anybody rich wants him to be.

But he wonders sometimes if maybe the rich look down on him. He wonders sometimes if maybe the rich think that just possibly they're a little bit *better* than him. The rich are always going to dinner parties and sneak previews. The rich have daughters at Princeton and sons in L.A. He knows the rich have swimming pools and security systems. He wonders what the rich would do if he and Velma knocked on their door one night. Would the rich let them in? Would they open the door wide and invite them in for crab? Or would they sic a slobbering Doberman on them? The rich are unpredictable.

The rich do not compare prices in the grocery stores or cut out coupons. The rich are rich enough to afford someone to do this for them, who, by working for the rich, does not feel at all compelled to check prices. No, the rich have their groceries bought for them by persons whose instructions do not include checking prices.

Mr. Pellisher, poor, lives with the constant thought that leg quarters at forty-nine cents per pound are cheaper than whole chickens at seventy-nine cents per pound, and even though he does not like dark meat, Mr. Pellisher must eat dark meat because he is not like the rich. That is to say that he is not rich. He figures the rich eat only breasts and pulley bones. The rich do not know the price of a can of Campbell's chicken noodle soup. The rich have no use for such knowledge.

How great Mr. Pellisher thinks this must be, to live in a world so high above the everyday human struggles of the race. The rich, for instance, never have to install spark plugs. The rich have never been stranded on the side of the road. The rich have never driven a wheezing '71 Ford Fairlane with a vibrating universal joint. Or put on brake shoes, tried to set points, suffered a burst radiator hose. They have never moaned and cursed on gravel flat on their collective rich backs with large rocks digging into their skin as they twisted greasy bolts into a greasy starter. The rich have it so easy.

The rich are saying something now. The rich are going on

vacation again. South of France? Wales? The rich have no conception of money. They have never bought a television or stereo on credit. They owe nothing to Sears. Their debutante daughters' braces were paid for with cash. The rich have unlimited credit which they do not need. In addition, the rich have never dug up septic tanks and seen with their own eyes the horrors contained there.

It appears that the rich are meeting other rich in June at Naples. From there they will fly to Angola. The ducks will darken the sky in late evening. The rich will doubtless shoot them with gold-plated Winchesters. The rich have never fired a Savage single-shot. The rich will go on to Ridder Creek in Alaska, where the salmon turn the water blood-red with their bodies. The rich have never seined minnows to impale upon hooks for pond bass. The rich do not camp out. The rich have never been inside a mobile home.

Mr. Pellisher has dreams of being rich. He plays Super Bingo at Kroger's. He goes inside and makes the minimum purchase twice a week, and gets the tickets. Each one could be the one. This is not the only thing he does. He also buys sweepstakes tickets and enters publishers' clearing house contests. But he never orders the magazines from the publishers. He does not affix the stamps. He has an uneasy feeling that the coupons from people who do not buy the magazines wind up at the bottom of the drawing barrel, but he has no way to prove this. He has no basis for this fear. It is unreasonable for him to think this. It is a phobia that has not yet been named.

The rich wish to have their matters taken care of immediately. They have their priorities in order. The rich have mixed-doubles sets to play. The rich have eighteen holes at two o'clock. Mr. Pellisher has taken to putting on the weekends and acquiring some of the equipment necessary for golfing. He watches the Masters' Classic and studies their pars and handicaps.

The rich are saying something else now. The rich wish to know which card Mr. Pellisher requires. The rich can produce MasterCharge, etc., upon request. The rich are logged and registered in computers all over the world. The wealth of the rich can be verified in an instant.

Mr. Pellisher has filled out all the needed forms. He has written down all the pertinent information. He has been helpful, courteous, polite, professional, warm, efficient, jovial, indulgent, cordial, ingratiating, familiar, benevolent. He has served the rich in the manner they are accustomed to. There is no outward indication of malice or loathing. But inside, in the deep gray portions of his mind where his secret thoughts lie, he hates the rich. What he'd really like to do is machine-gun the rich. Throttle the rich. He would like to see the great mansions of the rich burned down, their children limned in flame from the high windows. He would like to see the rich downtrodden, humbled, brought to their knees. He'd like to see the rich in rags. He'd like to see the rich on relief, or in prison. Arrested for smuggling cocaine. Fined for driving drunk. He'd like to see the rich suffer everything he ever suffered that all their money could heal.

But he knows it can never be so. He knows that the rich

can never be poor, that the poor can never be rich. He hates himself for being so nice to the rich. He knows the rich do not appreciate it. The rich merely expect it. The rich have become accustomed to it. He doubts the rich ever even think about it.

He tells none of this to the rich. He would like to, but he cannot. The rich might become offended. The rich might feel insulted. The rich might stop doing their business with him. Mr. Pellisher feeds off the rich. He sucks their blood, drawing it, little by little unto himself, a few dollars at a time, with never enough to satisfy his lust, slake his thirst.

The rich are leaving now. They are sliding onto their smooth leather seats, turning the keys in ignitions all over the world that set high-compression motors humming like well-fed cats. Their boats are docked and hosed down with fresh water. Their airplanes are getting refueled and restocked with liquor. Their accountants are preparing loopholes. Their lobsters are drowning in hot water, their caviar being chilled on beds of ice.

Mr. Pellisher waves to the rich as they pull away from the curb. But the rich don't look back.

OLD FRANK AND JESUS

Mr. Parker's on the couch, reclining. He's been there all morning, almost, trying to decide what to do.

Things haven't gone like he's planned. They never do.

The picture of his great-grandpa's on the mantel looking down at him, a framed old dead gentleman with a hat and a long beard who just missed the Civil War. The picture's fuzzy and faded, with this thing like a cloud coming up around his neck.

They didn't have good photography back then, Mr. P. thinks. That's why the picture looks like it does.

Out in the yard, his kids are screaming. They're just playing, but to Mr. P. it sounds like somebody's killing them. His wife's gone to the beauty parlor to get her hair fixed. There's a sick cow in his barn, but he hasn't been down to see about her this morning. He was up all night with her, just about. She's got something white and sticky running out from under her tail, and the vet's already been out three times without doing her any good. He charges for his visits anyway, though, twenty-five smacks a whack.

That's . . . seventy-five bucks, he thinks, and the old white stuff's just pouring out.

Mr. P. clamps his eyes shut and rolls over on the couch, feels it up. He had cold toast four hours ago. He needs to be up and out in the cotton patch, trying to pull the last bolls off the stalks, but the bottom's dropped out because foreign rayon's ruined the market. He guesses that somewhere across the big pond, little Japanese girls are sewing pants together and getting off from their jobs and meeting boyfriends for drinks and movies after work, talking about their supervisors. Maybe they're eating raw fish. They did that on Okinawa after they captured the place and everything settled down. He was on Okinawa. Mr. P. got shot on Okinawa.

He reaches down and touches the place, just above his knee. They were full of shit as a Christmas turkey. Eight hundred yards from the beach under heavy machine-gun fire. No cover. Wide open. They could have gotten some sun if they'd just been taking a vacation. They had palm trees. Sandy beaches. No lotion. No towels, no jamboxes, no frosty cool brewskies. They waded through water up to their necks and bullets zipped in the surf around them killing men and fish. Nobody had any dry cigarettes. Some of their men got run over by their own carriers and some of the boys behind shot the boys in front. Mr. P. couldn't tell who was shooting whom. He just shot. He stayed behind a concrete barrier for a while and saw some

Japanese symbols molded into the cement, but he couldn't read them. Every once in a while he'd stick his head out from behind the thing and just shoot.

He hasn't fired a shot in anger in years now, though. But he's thinking seriously about shooting a hole in the screen door with a pistol. Just a little hole.

He knows he needs to get up and go down to the barn and see about that cow, but he just can't face it today. He knows she won't be any better. She'll be just like she was last night, not touching the water he's drawn up in a barrel for her, not eating the hay he's put next to her. That's how it is with a cow when they get down, though. They just stay down. Even the vet knows that. The vet knows no shot he can give her will make her get up, go back on her feed. The vet's been to school. He's studied anatomy, biology. Other things, too. He knows all about animal husbandry and all.

But Mr. P. thinks him not much of a vet. The reason is, last year, Mr. P. had a stud colt he wanted cut, and he had him tied and thrown with a blanket over his head when the vet came out, and Mr. P. did most of the cutting, but the only thing the vet did was dance in and out with advice because he was scared of getting kicked.

The phone rings and Mr. P. stays on the couch and listens to it ring. It's probably somebody calling with bad news. That's about the only thing a phone's good for anyway, Mr. P. thinks, to let somebody get ahold of you with some bad news. He knows people just can't wait to tell bad news. Like if somebody dies, or if a man's cows are out in the road, somebody'll be sure to pick up the nearest phone and call somebody else and tell him or her all about it. And they'll tell other things, too. Personal things. Mr. P. thinks it'd probably be better to just not have a phone. If you didn't have a phone, they'd have to come over to your house personally to give you bad news, either drive over or walk. But with a phone, it's easy to give it to you. All they have to do's just pick it up and call, and there you are.

But on second thought, he thinks, if your house caught on fire and you needed to call up the fire department and report it, and you didn't have a phone, there you'd be again.

Or the vet.

The phone's still ringing. It rings eight or nine times. Just ringing ringing ringing. There's no telling who it is. It could be the FHA. They hold the mortgage on his place. Or, it could be the bank. They could be calling again to get real shitty about the note. He's borrowed money from them for seed and fertilizer and things and they've got a lien. And, it could be the county forester calling to tell him, Yes, Mr. Parker, it's just as we feared: your whole 160-acre tract of pine timber is heavily infested with the Southern pine beetle and you'll have to sell all your wood for stumpage and lose your shirt on the whole deal. It rings again. Mr. P. finally gets up from the couch and goes over to it. He picks it up. "Hello," he says.

"Hello?"

"Yes," Mr. P. says.

"Mr. Marvin Parker," the phone says.

"Speaking," says Mr. P.

"Jim Lyle calling, Mr. Parker. Amalgamated Pulpwood and

Benevolent Society? Just checking our records here and see you're a month behind on your premium. Just calling to check on the problem, Marv."

They always want their money, Mr. P. thinks. They don't care about you. They wouldn't give a damn if you got run over by a bush hog. They just want your money. Want you to pay that old premium.

"I paid," Mr. P. says. He can't understand it. "I pay by bank draft every month."

A little cough comes from the phone.

"Well yes," the voice says. "But our draft went through on a day when you were overdrawn, Mr. Parker."

Well kiss my ass, Mr. P. thinks.

Mr. P. can't say anything to this man. He knows what it is. His wife's been writing checks at the Fabric Center again. For material. What happened was, the girls needed dresses for the program at church, capes and wings and things. Plus, they had to spend $146.73 on a new clutch and pressure plate for the tractor. Mr. P. had to do all the mechanical stuff, pull the motor and all. Sometimes he couldn't find the right wrenches and had to hunt around in the dirt for this and that. There was also an unfortunate incident with a throw-out bearing.

Mr. P. closes his eyes and leans against the wall and wants to get back on the couch. Today, he just can't get enough of that couch.

"Can I borrow from the fund?" says Mr. P. He's never borrowed from the fund before.

"Borrow? Why. . . ."

"Would it be all right?" Mr. P. says.

"All right?"

"I mean would everything be fixed up?"

"Fixed up? You mean paid?" says the voice over the phone.

"Yes," says Mr. P. "Paid."

"Paid. Why, I suppose. . . ."

"Don't suppose," says Mr. P. He's not usually this ill with people like Jim Lyle of APABS. But he's sick of staying up with that cow every night. He's sick of his wife writing checks at the Fabric Center. He's sick of a vet who's scared of animals he's sworn to heal. He doesn't want Jim Lyle of APABS to suppose. He wants him to know.

"Well, yes sir, if that's the way. . . ."

"All right, then," Mr. P. says, and he hangs up the phone.

"Goodbye," he says, after he hangs it up. He goes back to the couch and stretches out quick, lets out this little groan. He puts one forearm over his eyes.

The kids are still screaming at the top of their lungs in the yard. He's worried about them being outside. There's been a rabies epidemic: foaming foxes and rabid raccoons running amuck. Even flying squirrels have attacked innocent people. And just last week, Mr. P. had to take his squirrel dog off, a little feist he had named Frank that was white with black spots over both eyes. He got him from a family of black folks down the road and they all swore up and down that his mama was a good one, had treed as many as sixteen in one morning. Mr. P. raised that dog from a puppy, played with him, fed him, let him sleep on his stomach and in front of the fire, and took him out in the summer with a dried squirrel skin and let him trail it all over the yard before he hung it up in a tree and let him tree it. He waited for old Frank to get a little older and then took him out the first frosty morning and shot a squirrel in front of him, didn't kill it on purpose, just wounded it, and let old Frank get ahold of it and get bitten in the nose because he'd heard all his life that doing that would make a squirrel dog every time if the dog had it in him. And old Frank did. He caught that squirrel and fought it all over the ground, squalling, with the squirrel balled up on his nose, bleeding, and finally killed it. After that he hated squirrels so bad he'd tree every squirrel he smelled. They killed nine opening day, one over the limit. Mr. P. was proud of old Frank.

But last week he took old Frank out in the pasture and shot him in the head with a .22 rifle because his wife said the rabies were getting too close to home.

Now why did I do that? Mr. P. wonders. Why did I let her talk me into shooting old Frank? I remember he used to come in here and lay down on my legs while I was watching "Dragnet." I'd pat him on the head and he'd close his eyes and curl up and just seem happy as anything. He'd even go to sleep sometimes, just sleep and sleep. And he wouldn't mess in the house either. Never did. He'd scratch on the door till somebody let him out. Then he'd come back in and hop up here and go to sleep.

Mr. P. feels around under the couch to see if it's still there. It is. He just borrowed it a few days ago, from his neighbor,

Hulet Steele. He doesn't even know if it'll work. But he figures it will. He told Hulet he wanted it for rats. He told Hulet he had some rats in his corncrib.

Next thing he knows, somebody's knocking on the front door. Knocking hard, like he can't even see the kids out in the yard and send them in to call him out. He knows who it probably is, though. He knows it's probably Hereford Mullins, another neighbor, about that break in the fence, where his cows are out in the road. Mr. P. knows the fence is down. He knows his cows are out in the road, too. But he just can't seem to face it today. It seems like people just won't leave him alone.

He doesn't much like Hereford Mullins anyway. Never has. Not since that night at the high school basketball game when their team won and Hereford Mullins tried to vault over the railing in front of the seats and landed on both knees on the court, five feet straight down, trying to grin like it didn't hurt.

Mr. P. thinks he might just get up and go out on the front porch and slap the shit out of Hereford Mullins. He gets up and goes out there.

It's Hereford, all right. Mr. P. stops inside the screen door. The kids are still screaming in the yard, getting their school clothes dirty. Any other time they'd be playing with old Frank. But old Frank can't play with them now. Old Frank's busy getting his eyeballs picked out right now probably by some buzzards down in the pasture.

"Ye cows out in the road again," says Hereford Mullins. "Thought I'd come up here and tell ye."

"All right," says Mr. P. "You told me."

"Like to hit em while ago," says Hereford Mullins. "I'd git em outa the road if they's mine."

"I heard you the first time," says Mr. P.

"Feller come along and hit a cow in the road," goes on Hereford Mullins, "he ain't responsible. Cows ain't sposed to be in the road. Sposed to be behind a fence."

"Get off my porch," says Mr. P.

"What?"

"I said get your stupid ass off my porch," Mr. P. says.

Hereford kind of draws up, starts to say something, but leaves the porch huffy. Mr. P. knows he'll be the owner of a dead cow within two minutes. That'll make two dead cows, counting the one in the barn not quite dead yet that he's already out seventy-five simoleans on.

He goes back to the couch.

Now there'll be a lawsuit, probably. Herf'll say his neck's hurt, or his pickup's hurt, or something else. Mr. P. reaches under the couch again and feels it again. It's cold and hard, feels scary.

Mr. P.'s never been much of a drinking man, but he knows there's some whiskey in the kitchen cabinet. Sometimes when the kids get colds or the sore throat, he mixes up a little whiskey and lemon juice and honey and gives it to them in a teaspoon. That and a peppermint stick always helps their throats.

He gets the whiskey, gets a little drink, and then gets another pretty good drink. It's only ten o'clock. He should have had a lot of work done by now. Any other time he'd be out on the tractor or down in the field or up in the woods cutting firewood.

Unless it was summer. If it was summer he'd be out in the garden picking butter beans or sticking tomatoes or cutting hay or fixing fences or working on the barn roof or digging up the septic tank or swinging a joe-blade along the driveway or cultivating the cotton or spraying or trying to borrow some more money to buy some more poison or painting the house or cutting the grass or doing a whole bunch of other things he doesn't want to do anymore at all. All he wants to do now's stay on the couch.

Mr. P. turns over on the couch and sees the picture of Jesus on the wall. It's been hanging up there for years. Old Jesus, he thinks. Mr. P. used to know Jesus. He used to talk to Jesus all the time. There was a time when he could have a little talk with Jesus and everything'd be all right. Four or five years ago he could. Things were better then, though. You could raise cotton and hire people to pick it. They even used to let the kids out of school to pick it. Not no more, though. Only thing kids wanted to do now was grow long hair and listen to the damn Beatles.

Mr. P. knows about hair because he cuts it in his house. People come in at night and sit around the fire in his living room and spit tobacco juice on the hearth and Mr. P. cuts their hair. He talks to them about cotton and cows and shuffles, clockwise and counterclockwise around the chair they're sitting in, in his house shoes and undershirt and overalls and snips here and there.

Most of the time they watch TV, "Gunsmoke" or "Perry Mason." Sometimes they watch Perry Como. And *some*times, they'll get all involved and interested in a show and stay till the show's over.

One of Mr. P.'s customers—this man who lives down the road and doesn't have a TV—comes every Wednesday night to get his haircut. But Mr. P. can't cut much of his hair, having to cut it every week like that. He has to just snip the scissors around on his head some and make out like he's cutting it, comb it a little, walk around his head a few times, to make him think he's getting a real haircut. This man always comes in at 6:45 P.M., just as Mr. P. and his family are getting up from the supper table.

This man always walks up, and old Frank used to bark at him when he'd come up in the yard. It was kind of like a signal that old Frank and Mr. P. had, just between them. But it wasn't a secret code or anything. Mr. P. would be at the supper table, and he'd hear old Frank start barking, and if it was Wednesday night, he'd know to get up from the table and get his scissors. The Hillbillies always come on that night at seven, and it takes Mr. P. about fifteen minutes to cut somebody's hair.

This man starts laughing at the opening credits of the Hillbillies, and shaking his head when it shows old Jed finding his black gold, his Texas tea, just as Mr. P.'s getting through with his head. So by the time he's finished, the Hillbillies have already been on for one or two minutes. And then, when Mr. P. unpins the bedsheet around this man's neck, if there's nobody else sitting in his living room watching TV or waiting for a haircut, this man just stays in the chair, doesn't get up, and says, "I bleve I'll jest set here and watch the Hillbillies with ya'll since they already started if ya'll don't care."

It's every Wednesday night's business.

Mr. P. doesn't have a license or anything, but he actually does more than a regular barber would do. For one thing, he's got some little teenincy scissors he uses to clip hairs out of folks' noses and ears. Plus, Mr. P.'s cheaper than the barbers in town. Mr. P.'ll lower your ears for fifty cents. He doesn't do shaves, though. He's got shaky hands. He couldn't shave a balloon or anything. He could flat shave the damn Beatles though.

Mr. P.'s wondering when the school bus will come along. It's late today. What happened was, Johnny Crawford got it stuck in a ditch about a mile down the road trying to dodge one of Mr. P.'s cows. They've called for the wrecker, though, on Mr. P.'s phone. They gave out that little piece of bad news over his phone, and he thinks he heard the wrecker go down the road a while ago. He knows he needs to get up and go down there and fix that fence, get those cows up, but he doesn't think he will. He thinks he'll just stay right here on the couch and drink a little more of this whiskey.

Mr. P. would rather somebody get him down on the ground and beat his ass like a drum than to have to fix that fence. The main thing is, he doesn't have anybody to help him. His wife has ruined those kids of his, spoiled them, until the oldest boy, fourteen, can't even tie his own shoelaces. Mr. P. can say something to him, tell him to come on and help him go do something for a minute, and he'll act like he's deaf and dumb. And if he does go, he whines and moans and groans and carries on about it until Mr. P. just sends him on back to the house so he won't have to listen to it. Mr. P. can see now that he messed up with his kids a long time ago. He's been too soft on them. They don't even know what work is. It just amazes Mr. P. He wasn't raised like that. He had to work when he was little. And it was rough as an old cob back then. Back then you couldn't sit around on your ass all day long and listen to a bunch of long-haired hippies singing a bunch of rock and roll on the radio.

Mr. P.'s even tried paying his kids to get out and help him work, but they won't do it. They say he doesn't pay enough. Mr. P.'s raised such a rebellious bunch of youngsters with smart mouths that they'll even tell him what the minimum wage is.

Even if his oldest boy would help him with the fence, it'd still be an awful job. First off they'd have to move all the cows to another pasture so they could tear the whole fence down and do it right. And the only other pasture Mr. P.'s got available is forty acres right next to his corn patch. They'd probably push the fence down and eat his corn up while he's across the road putting up the new fence, because his wife won't run cows. Mr. P.'s run cows and run cows and tried to get his wife out there to help him run cows and she won't hardly run cows at all. She's not fast enough to head one off or anything. Plus, she's scared of cows. She's always afraid she's going to stampede them and get run over by a crazed cow. About the only thing Mr. P.'s wife is good for when it comes to running cows is just sort of jumping around, two or three feet in any direction, waving her arms, and hollering, "Shoo!"

Mr. P. can't really think of a whole lot his wife *is* good for except setting his kids against him. It seems like they've fought him at every turn, wanting to buy new cars and drive up to Memphis to shop and getting charge accounts at one place and another and wanting him to loan money to her old drunk brother. Mr. P. doesn't know what the world's coming to. They've got another damn war started now and they'll probably be wanting his boys to go over there in a few more years and get killed or at the very least get their legs blown off. Mr. P. worries about that a good bit. But Mr. P. just worries about everything, really. Just worries all the time. There's probably not a minute that goes by when he's awake that he's not worrying about something. It's kind of like a weight he's carrying around with him that won't get off and can't get off because there's no way for it *to* get off.

The whiskey hasn't done him any good. He hoped it would, but he really knew that it wouldn't. Mr. P. thinks he knows the only thing that'll do him any good, and it won't be good.

He wonders what his wife'll say when she comes in and sees him still on the couch. Just him and Jesus, and grandpa. She's always got something to say about everything. About the only thing she doesn't say too much about is that guy who sells the siding. Mr. P.'s come up out of the pasture on the tractor four or five times and seen that guy coming out of the house after trying to sell some siding to his wife. She won't say much about him, though. She just says he's asking for directions.

Well, there the bus is to get his kids. Mr. P. can hear it pull up and he can hear the doors open. He guesses they got it out of the ditch all right. He could have taken his tractor down there and maybe pulled it out, but he might not have. A man has to be careful on a tractor. Light in the front end like they are, a man has to be careful how he hooks onto something.

Especially something heavy like a school bus. But the school bus is leaving now. Mr. P. can hear it going down the road.

It's quiet in the house now.

Yard's quiet, too.

If old Frank was in here now he'd be wanting out. Old Frank. Good little old dog. Just the happiest little thing you'd ever seen. He'd jump clean off the ground to get a biscuit out of your hand. He'd jump about three feet high. And just wag that stubby tail hard as he could.

Old Frank.

Mr. P. thinks now maybe he should have just shot his wife instead of old Frank when she first started talking about shooting old Frank. Too late now.

Mr. P. gets another drink of the whiskey and sees Jesus looking down at him. He feels sorry for Jesus. Jesus went through a lot to save sinners like him. Mr. P. thinks, Jesus died to save me and sinners like me.

Mr. P. can see how it was that day. He figures it was hot. In a country over there like that, it was probably always hot. And that cross He had to carry was heavy. He wonders if Jesus cried from all the pain they put Him through. Just thinking about anybody being so mean to Jesus that He'd cry is enough to make Mr. P. want to cry. He wishes he could have been there to help Jesus that day. He'd have helped Him, too. If he could have known what he knows now, and could have been there that day, he'd have tried to rescue Jesus. He could have fought some of the soldiers off. But there were probably so many of them, he wouldn't have had a chance. He'd have fought for Him, though. He'd have fought for Jesus harder than he'd ever fought for anything in his life, harder than he fought on the beach at Okinawa. Given his own blood. Maybe he could have gotten his hands on a sword, and kept them away from Jesus long enough for tHem to get away. But those guys were probably good sword-fighters back then. Back then they probably practiced a lot. It wouldn't have mattered to him, though. He'd have given his blood, all of it, and gladly to help Jesus.

The kids are all gone now. Old Frank's gone. His wife's still at the beauty parlor. She won't be in for a while. He gets another drink of the whiskey. It's awful good. He hates to stop drinking it, but he hates to keep on. With Jesus watching him and all.

The clock's ticking on the mantel. The hair needs sweeping off the hearth. He knows that cow's still got that white stuff running out from under her tail. But somebody else'll just have to see about it. Maybe the guy who sells the siding can see about it.

Mr. P. figures he ought to make sure it'll work first, so he pulls it out from under the couch and points it at the screen door in back. Right through the kitchen.

He figures maybe they won't be able to understand that. It'll be a big mystery that they'll never figure out. Some'll say Well he was making sure it'd work. Others'll say Aw it might have been there for years. They'll say What was he doing on the couch? And, I guess we'll have to go to town for a haircut now.

They'll even talk about how he borrowed it from Hulet for rats.

Old Frank has already gone through this. He didn't understand it. He trusted Mr. P. and knew he'd never hurt him. Maybe Mr. P. was a father to him. Maybe Mr. P. was God to him. What could he have been thinking of when he shot his best friend?

What in God's name can he be thinking of now?

Mr. Parker, fifty-eight, is reclining on his couch.

BOY AND DOG

The dog was already dead.
He was in the road.
A kid watched behind trees.
Tears shone on his face.
He dashed into the road.
Then a car came along.
He retreated to the sidewalk.
He heard his mother calling.
More cars were coming now.
The dog was really dead.
Blood was on the asphalt.
He could see it puddling.
The hubcap was bloody too.
It was also badly dented.
It came off a Mustang.

He ran to the dog.
A car drove up fast.
He caught up the tail.
He pulled on the dog.
It slid in slick blood.
The car got even closer.
He dropped it and ran.
His mother called to him.
She was on the porch.
Johnny what are you doing?
She couldn't see him crying.
His Spam was getting cold.
Bozo was the dog's name.
Bozo was an old dog.
The boy was only eight.
Bozo would be eleven forever.
He ran back to Bozo.
Then he pulled Bozo closer.
But another car came along.
It was the killer Mustang.
It was hunting its hubcap.
The boy had seen it.
He picked up a brick.
The driver was going slow.
He looked out the window.
He really wanted that hubcap.
It was a '65 fastback.
It was worth some money.

It had bad main seals.
Black oil leaked each night.
The dipstick was always low.
It had clobbered the dog.
The wheel hit him hard.
The shiny hubcap said BONG!
The kid held his brick.
He was hiding behind trees.
The driver was slowing down.
It was around here somewhere.
The brick was antique lemon.
It had three round holes.
But it was still heavy.
The car got awful close.
The kid held his brick.
The guy turned his head.
He didn't see the kid.
The kid threw the brick.
It landed on his head.
The driver fell over unconscious.
He jammed the gas down.
The Mustang burned some rubber.
It also burned some oil.
A big tree stopped it.
The tree shook pretty hard.
The windshield shattered in spiderwebs.
The horn started blowing loud.
The guy's head was down.

The horn blew and blew.
The kid got really panicky.
He ran out to help.
He had always loved dogs.
He grabbed the tail again.
The dog was pretty heavy.
The blood made him slide.
The kid kept looking around.
Something popped under the hood.
A little smoke rolled up.
The horn was still blowing.
Wires popped and something crackled.
Then the smoke turned black.
The kid got his dog.
The dog was messed up.
One of his eyes protruded.
Tire tracks were on him.
He was starting to stiffen.
All right then young man.
I'll put these Doritos up.
She didn't hear him yelling.
He couldn't yell very loud.
She went back to lunch.
The smoke wasn't bad yet.
The kid ran back across.
The horn was still blowing.
It was weaker than before.
The battery was getting tired.

Flames leaped under the car.
The guy blew the horn.
He looked sort of dead.
He had this big hole.
It was in his head.
The yellow flames went WHOOSH!
Then the paint started burning.
It was really getting hot.
Nobody would want it now.
The guy's hair was curling.
Fire was coming out everywhere.
The gas tank blew up.
There was this big explosion.
It knocked the kid down.
The car rocked with it.
Two of the tires blew.
The car sat lower then.
The kid said oh shit.
He regretted throwing the brick.
He touched the door handle.
Some of his skin melted.
His fingerprints were instantly gone.
It didn't hurt a bit.
He knew it should have.
It scared him pretty bad.
He could hear music playing.
He rubbed his melted hand.
The guy's hair was gone.

Smoke was thick and black.
It choked him something awful.
He coughed and gagged some.
He ran across the road.
He was needing the telephone.
The emergency number was 911.
He learned it in school.
His class visited the firemen.
They mentioned playing with matches.
They didn't mention throwing bricks.
He ran fast toward home.
But halfway there he stopped.
He didn't have enough time.
He had to go back.
The Mustang had turned black.
The tires were burning off.
Coils of wire fell away.
It wasn't worth much now.
The guy's shirt was burning.
The kid could smell it.
It looked like an Izod.
People were pulled over gawking.
One man came running up.
He was evidently a hero.
A shirt swaddled his hands.
The man grabbed the door.
The hero screamed a little.
The door handle had him.

It wouldn't turn him loose.
The fire rolled around him.
It started curling his hair.
He tried rescuing the driver.
The driver was buckled up.
He was also shoulder-harnessed.
The hero finally got loose.
But he screamed a lot.
His clothes were smoking bad.
He fell and rolled over.
The grass was scorched black.
He was beating himself silly.
His arm had turned black.
The kid watched all this.
The hero flailed the grass.
Somebody needed to get help.
But of course nobody did.
Some people won't get involved.
The car was fully involved.
It wasn't worth twenty bucks.
The motor was probably okay.
The aluminum transmission had melted.
The hero was still screaming.
Suddenly they heard an airhorn.
A big red truck arrived.
Firemen jumped off the truck.
They started hollering Jesus Christ.
One fireman hollered holy shit!

The driver was pretty nervous.
It was his first run.
He didn't set the brake.
The nozzlemen pulled the hose.
They were ready for water.
They were holding it tight.
The driver engaged the pump.
This disengaged the rear wheels.
Nozzlemen were screaming for water.
The hose was pulled away.
The truck was rolling backwards.
The firemen were chasing it.
They were really yelling loud.
It rolled into a ditch.
It was a deep ditch.
It was really a canal.
The canal held deep water.
The truck was pointing up.
The motor had already quit.
They couldn't pump any water.
The hoses wouldn't work now.
The Mustang driver got smaller.
The kid took it in.
He looked for the brick.
It was under the Mustang.
He tried to get it.
He thought about his fingerprints.
But he didn't have any.

So he let it go.
The firemen were screaming loud.
One had sense and radioed.
A crowd of spectators gathered.
A van with newsmen arrived.
There was an anchorman inside.
They started setting up cameras.
The announcer straightened his tie.
The Mustang was solid black.
The fire department came running.
They carried some powdered extinguishers.
They weighed almost twenty pounds.
They started mashing the handles.
White clouds of chemicals rolled.
Fire flashed here and there.
People coughed and almost gagged.
The gas tank kept burning.
They couldn't put it out.
They ran out of powder.
It was only baking soda.
Most people don't know that.
Firemen make money servicing them.
These had steak suppers sometimes.
They played bingo and drank.
Once they had a party.
Some of them got drunk.
Then they had a run.
Their food was barbecued goat.

But the goat burned up.
So did the Mustang driver.
The other truck came then.
A captain of firemen arrived.
He issued orders and radioed.
They stretched lines and attacked.
Only one tire was burning.
Bystanders muttered about their incompetence.
The firemen were pretty embarrassed.
An ambulance pulled up next.
The firemen acted very important.
They bullied the ambulance attendants.
They pried open the door.
One joked about Crispy Critters.
This is a breakfast cereal.
The captain's face turned red.
He began questioning some witnesses.
The kid sidled off unobtrusively.
His Spam was still waiting.
He went to the dog.
The dog was getting stiff.
He picked up one leg.
It stayed up like that.
He looked at the car.
A wrecker was driving up.
He'd never seen a wrecker.
He stuck around to watch.
The anchorman made eyewitness reports.

Several people were interrogated live.
They rushed home to brag.
They were almost real celebrities.
They would phone their neighbors.
They would phone their friends.
Neighbors and friends would watch.
The almost-celebrities would celebrate.
The parties would be gay.
The kid would see them.
He would recognize them all.
It would all be over.
Johnny Carson would come on.
He would be safe forever.
He would request a puppy.
His father would deny him.
He would make different promises.
His daddy would say no.
There were licenses and fees.
Puppies always grew into dogs.
And dogs sometimes chased cars.
And cars sometimes killed dogs.
And bricks sometimes got thrown.
Boys still go to woodsheds.
But fathers must be cautious.
Kids are violent these days.
Especially where pets are concerned.

JULIE: A MEMORY

It was muddy where we parked and I had to be careful not to get on soft ground. That's just a blank space. When I tried to touch her, she slapped my hands away. I heard him slip the safety off. "I don't want you to if you don't want to," she said. Then we went inside. I don't know why I drove all the way through. She didn't say. And then Julie came in. I figured that would make her happy. She had some kind of a fit all of a sudden. "Lock the doors," she said. He had the wrench up in one hand and his fingers were greasy and black and trembling. I didn't want to tell her. We got inside and we sat down. The blood had scabbed on my face. "Don't," she said. I crawled on my hands and knees to the first one just as he picked up the rifle. She wanted popcorn. You see all this stuff on TV now about abortions, and once I saw a doctor holding a fetus in his fingers. She'd left me some sandwich stuff in the refrigerator. I got dressed and turned off all the lights and locked the door. I don't know how many times he hit me. She didn't want to. She said that everything was a mistake, that she didn't love me. He begged hard for his life. And for no reason then, he just slapped her. When I thought of all that, I started feeling good. He looked like he was half asleep. The first boy pulled her panties down around her knees and she whimpered. They say they don't cook their hamburgers ahead of time, but they do. There was a little road that ran back behind, where all the black people were buried. I'd have to hunt under the seat for my socks. "Don't open it," she said. I wiped it with my hand and looked at it. But I wasn't really sure. Then he grabbed her legs, panting, and spread them apart. We lost track of time. I could have reached out and grabbed it. I recognized the second boy. He slapped her so hard her face leaped around sideways. Everybody has to have love. And it seemed like it ruined everything. But that car was there again. It happened quickly. What Julie and I were doing was no different. It was an adventure story. I think I said please to him that night. You can't ask things like that. I didn't even know if we could live together. But I knew she'd be on my side anyway. I worried about it for a long time, that I'd get caught. But I knew we had to try. I didn't want to turn his soul loose if he wasn't ready, so I told him to pray. It's a big step. He had a motor jack set up in front of the grill. One of them said that he didn't have any matches. Houses were all around. I had to keep my shirt on in front of my mother so she wouldn't see the scratches on my back. I stopped outside the city limits and got us a beer from the trunk.

She wasn't showing yet. I was trying to get up but I felt like I was drunk. I didn't figure he was ready. "Open that door, " he said. I got up on my knees. I'd been planning on staying overnight with some friends at the spillway, but it started raining hard about ten o'clock and we didn't want to sleep in our cars, so we just went home. When we'd first started doing it, we'd always used rubbers. I'd put off telling Mother. And it was driving him nuts. He jammed the rifle against my head. I wanted to go for pizza. Just his feet were sticking out from under the car. She said he was always buying her coffee and eating his lunch with her. I didn't say too much. We were quiet for a while then. I was wet with mud and it was cold on my legs. None of that mattered. And then she got pregnant. Trying to get her hot. So I just kept my mouth shut. I thought they were going to kill us. I listened. But she didn't even say anything about it. I thought we were going to talk. "Somebody with car trouble, I guess," I said. I think my mother wanted to ask me why I wasn't going with Julie anymore, but she didn't. We finally got out there, and the woods were dark and wet. She had her hands up in front of her face. I've even seen her in bars. It was so clear when it was happening. It didn't change anything. "I don't want no part of it," he said. Once we did it right there on the couch with her mother in the next room. I knew I had done the right thing. The first one handed the rifle to the second one and pushed her dress up. I could never go over there without thinking about all those dead people under the stones. Finally it was over. I didn't know if it would work. I put my face between her breasts and closed my eyes and just laid there. If we weren't doing it we were talking about doing it. I finished my beer and then got back in the car. He wanted to know who it was but I didn't say anything. "Thanks," she said. I didn't want to marry her. The road was wet so I drove carefully. It's not something you should do without thinking about it. She said he loved to dance. I cranked it and we sat hugging each other until it warmed up. Before she got out of the car, I made her tell me where he lived. She chain-smoked cigarettes and had brown stains on her fingertips. I wondered if maybe she'd had a child born out of wedlock herself. "Don't," she said. "Please don't." I thought, If you were married to her, you could do this all the time. Mother had offered to buy some for me, but I told her I wanted to take care of things like that by myself. I didn't want to embarrass her. She was talking about baby showers and baby clothes. I could see the rifle lying there, pointing toward the road. Her mother was strange to me. We started dressing. "Hurry up," she'd say. "Hurry up and get it in me." There was something about it on the news. He had his finger on the trigger. His soul was what I thought about, and mine, too. Her mother looked up when I went in, but then she turned away, back to the television. She had mud all over her face and she didn't want me to look at her. There was another boy standing in the rain, watching me. "I love you, " she said. They had her tied when I came to. I had to go home finally. He didn't hear me walk up to the car. The porch light was on when we pulled in and neither of us said anything. I figured she'd probably scream. I wiped my forearm across my eyes. He was probably about twenty. Maybe it wasn't even my baby. "When you going to tell your mother?" she said. I didn't know what I was going to tell my mother. You could hear that rain drumming on the roof while you were taking your clothes off and then when you were naked together on the backseat, with the doors locked, it was just the best thing you could want. Down behind the fence there were squirrels and deer. They used to live beside her. I didn't know what to do. Give up my whole life for her and the baby? I walked up on the porch and knocked on the door and heard her mother tell me to come in. I got her in my car and the first thing she did was pull my hand up her dress. She wasn't rude, but I could see that she just didn't want to talk. By then I couldn't do anything. He must have brought the whiskey because she never kept liquor in the house. "You bout two seconds away from gettin a bullet through your head," he said. But I wasn't ready to marry her. Then she squatted down, like she was going to pee on the ground. It was where we always went. She said she didn't want to get married. We held hands. "Ya'll done lost your fuckin minds," he said. "I want to," I said. It was cold outside. I parked my car in the woods and walked back down the road quickly, then went over a barbed-wire fence and down through a pasture. I know he was thinking about that night and what he'd done to us. She had her hand on my dick. I looked at Julie. "Don't," she said. That woman always seemed so hurt. I didn't know what to say. "Hell, she wants it," he said. We'd rest for ten minutes, kissing, and then we'd start again. I wanted to tell my mother and ask her what I should do. We pulled out finally and headed out of town. This night was a night we were

going to talk. I thought I was going to wreck the car. You can't
do without it. I couldn't see anything. We talked some more.
She'd take her nails and scrape me so hard I'd almost tell her to
stop. The rifle fell into the mud. "What are you waiting on?"
she said. I got to be an expert at getting fully dressed sitting
down. I was afraid she'd get up and walk in there and see us
on the couch, but it didn't stop us. The first boy had her by the
arms and he was dragging her toward a tree. "Tell her to open
the door," he said. I'd always thought that having kids was
something you should give some thought to. There's nothing
blacker than woods at night. You could have her whenever you
wanted her. There were a lot of people on the square when I cut
through. She unbuckled my belt and unzipped my pants. We ate
in the parking lot. We had to hurry because the movie was about
to start. And then we said we didn't care what it was as long as
it was healthy. When I went to bed, I pulled the covers all the
way up over my head and saw it all again, every word and every
sound and every raindrop. I didn't want her to have an abortion.
I guess it was kind of like when you're little, and you've done
something your mother or your father is going to whip you for,
but you're hoping that if you beg hard enough they won't. I
rolled the window down. He ran off into the woods with a crazy
little cry. I got up quickly and went to meet her. "You get out of
that car," the boy with the rifle said. He sounded drunk. I took
a drink of it. I like adventure. It surprised me when she said she
did. I think she felt guilty about the night we got rained out on
our fishing trip. She slid up on the console next to me and we
left. The second one turned around and looked at me with his

dick sticking out of his pants. She laid her head back down. I couldn't understand why they were doing what they were doing. She pushed her dress up and pulled my hand in between her legs. I tried to talk to her for a while, but it was never any use. She got to telling me all about her job, and how this man who worked there was always trying to sweet-talk her on break. I had an old pistol that had belonged to my father. She said leave it alone. I had some beer iced down in my car and I asked her if she wanted one. Or three. "Get out," the one with the rifle said. She did say that Julie would be ready in a few minutes. I sat in the driveway for a long time just looking at the house. The one I hit got up off the ground. People were watching television within sight of us. I was running late when I got home, but she had my clothes ironed and laid out for me. It couldn't have been easy for her. I'd thought he was hurting her because of the way she was moaning. I went inside quietly and washed the blood off my face with a wet towel. They had a nice home there, but he was a long way from the house. I romped on it a little and the back end slid. She said if I wanted to take care of her, take her home. Something cold touched the side of my head. "Please, God," he said. I asked her what she would do about her clothes. When it was dry we'd take a blanket out of the trunk and spread it on the ground. The first thing she did was go over to the boy and spit on him. I knew we'd have a good time. She always made me lock the doors. I couldn't understand why nobody was coming to help us. "Listen," I said, "I don't know what you guys want." I could tell that she was happy. But one night we ran out or I forgot to buy some,

or something. It didn't have a jack under it anywhere. The
dates were so faded, and the names, too, that you couldn't read
them. She didn't know the third one. Sometimes we'd tear each
other's clothes getting them off. She told me on the way home.
I knew the leaves were wet and cold and I knew how they felt
on her skin. She raised up and looked at me. The tires were
spinning in the mud. But then I thought that maybe she was
just lonely. "You want to do it up here?" I said. "Or you want
to get in the back?" But we were running late. She was on her
knees and I could see him lunging at her face. I asked her if
we were finished and she said yes. We'd have to find a place to
live. I didn't want it growing up with just its mother's name,
either. She had enough on her already. She was like me. I could
have let him live. There were cars passing on the road and I
kept thinking that one would surely pull in. I didn't even know
where Julie's daddy was. There was a fifth of Wild Turkey on
the kitchen table. I used to hunt there. He put his hands up in
front of his face and closed his eyes and said, "Jesus, Jesus, oh
please Jesus." The night I came in from fishing, I went to bed
quietly and tried to go to sleep, but I could hear them moving
in her bed, and once in a while, her moaning. But she got
up that night and put on a robe and told me it was all right.
I was afraid it would hurt her too much. I could do it, too.
I just wanted her to be happy. The only thing we could think
about was getting it into her as quickly as possible. I loved that
rain. She said, "If I could dance, I'd marry that man." I was
hungry and wanted to fix myself some breakfast. Some were
killed in the Civil War. Blood was in my eyes. You could see

the ruts deep in the mud where the tires had gone before us. That night was no different. I took her blouse and bra off and she got on top of me. I told her that I wanted to take care of her. He was gone the next morning and we didn't talk about it. I said I hoped it was a boy. "You just shut your mouth," he said. I thought about it. His eyes didn't close. Give me a good old love story anytime. It was one of those space movies. The foot of the fetus was smaller than his thumb. It was just like shooting a dog. I yelled for him as loud as I could. The first boy went around and tried to open the door. I made a decision right there on that backseat, naked, holding her. Julie drew up and leaned against her side of the car. I didn't say anything. My mother would be a grandmother. "You can't hide it forever," I said. But sometimes when you do things, you have to pay for them. She had on a red dress and white shoes. She had already gone somewhere, on a date, I guess. Almost all of her friends were married and she wasn't used to dating and she probably worried over what I thought about it. I went into her room and I woke her up. I thought about it. I don't know how long we did it that night. It seemed like that broke the ice. There was blood dripping off my face. It made everything seem so nice. "What do you think?" she said. You can't place your order and pull on around and have it ready within thirty seconds without having it cooked ahead of time. She was two months pregnant. So I went out there and got her one. His hands relaxed and one of his feet kicked. They have to. But it was only a matter of time. "We don't want any trouble," I said. On that backseat with her I felt I had all the happiness I'd ever need. They had her tied on the ground with her arms around a tree. In Memphis. All this is fuzzy. I had to keep wiping the blood out of my eyes. Mother stays gone all the time. I couldn't tell her. It had already been in all the papers about the boy they found. Maybe even me. He stomped on my head. The third boy was still standing in the road. I remember he just rolled over and pulled the covers up over him. We'd taken all kinds of crazy chances. She said what was done was done. His face was down in the mud. I'm for life. There weren't any napkins and they didn't give us enough ketchup. "You told her?" I said. She said think about it. She hadn't come right out and said it. Nobody wants to. I eased it up into park and got out with my hands up. It had taken her a long time to get over Daddy leaving her, but she was beginning to make the most of it. It was sharp. They must have known I was there. "You kids have a good time," her mother said. I asked her if she wanted to go to the police or the hospital or what. I don't know how we got over in the woods. Julie wasn't anywhere around. She told it like she was in a trance. There were junked cars all over the pasture. "Just tell me what you want me to do," I said. "If you want this car you can have it." We'd get so hot we just wouldn't think clearly. He'd laid the rifle down. I just unlocked the door and went on into the kitchen. I knew he'd hurt her. "Please," I said, "don't hurt her." He was trying to pull the motor out of a '68 Camaro down in the pasture. I think my mind has tried to cover it up some way. "Please," he said. "Please please please." It wasn't that bad. I didn't think anything about it. "What's wrong?" she said. They had homemade tombstones, carved out of sandrock. I didn't want to hurt her. The first one was doing something to her. The glass was fogged over with our breathing. My car was over there. I didn't want to get up. I couldn't see her getting an abortion. It was pretty good. The first one was puking against a tree. It's a hell of a thing, to see your mother doing that. "Would you just hold me for a little while?" I said. The gun went off. "What?" I said. The one who kicked me put a knife against my throat and I didn't do anything else. "Then we'll tell yours," she said. But I probably wasn't the only kid who'd ever seen something like that. I just had gotten my car paid for, but it needed new tires. It squealed once in the road and was gone. He didn't want to die. I got out to take a leak and the ground was soft. When I grabbed for it, the other one kicked me. The vinyl top was rotted. He screamed when he came. And I wondered what she'd say. They must have heard my car pull up. She wouldn't even look up from the TV when I said something. "Are you sure?" she said. I cared about her. "I'm sure," I said. He rolled out from under it with a wrench in his hand and a pissed-off look on his face, and he knew me then. It was a green '72 Camaro with a black top. He slammed me against the fender. He dropped the wrench. "Don't ask me any questions, " I said. "Just hold me." I didn't know if I loved her. "You having trouble?" I said. I thought my nose was running. She was watching "Knot's Landing" and I watched it with her for a while. Randy Hillhouse lived not an eighth of a mile away. I missed Daddy, sure. "Remember me?" I said. I wound up getting about half fucked-up in the kitchen before I got my sausage and eggs fried. "We won't be out late," she

said. It was the muzzle of a .22 rifle. I knew she wanted me
to marry her. "I wonder what that's doing there," she said. I
thought I'd seen the boy somewhere before. Julie was quiet.
I went down like I'd been shot. "Oh, man, no," he said. It
was raining, not hard, just enough to where you had to keep
the wipers going to see. The movie wasn't that great. I could
have let it go, I guess. We never did it less than twice. I've
seen hogs do like that. I stuck it in his face. After it was over,
we held each other for a long time. Later on I remembered it
like a nightmare. It seems like I cried. Every night. I wanted a
cigarette and couldn't smoke in there. She won't even talk to me
now, doesn't act like she remembers who I am. "You told her?"
I said. I didn't love her. Pow! I think now that I must have been
trying to choke him. We'd talked about telling her. But I loved
my mother. The first one and the second one were brothers.
About the same age as me. I turned and looked at it. "It's okay
to cry sometimes," she said. The car was parked at the end
of the turnaround. I could see this kid in my mind, running
around on a softball field. "You want to tell her?" I said. When
I pulled the door shut, I thought about it and unlocked it and
stepped inside the living room and turned on the lamp. It's
more like a dream now that never really happened. She was
screaming for me to help her. She hadn't held me like that in
a long time. I waited a week. Her mouth tasted like chewing
gum. I think I cried some. It got hard again. I'd already put it
up in reverse when the first one knocked on the window. We
kissed. I was late when I got over there. I must have passed
out. She kissed me, and then she looked at her mother. "For

God's sake," I said. I only put one shell in it. I always felt like
her mother knew what we were doing. We'd have clothes lying
everywhere. I remember one time I walked in on them when
they were in bed. I made sure it was him. "You can talk to me
anytime you want to," she said. I can't forget how he looked
lying there. She said take her home. There was a strange car
in the driveway when I pulled up. It was about fifteen miles
from town. I stopped and watched for a long time before I went
up. They were waiting for us. I thought I was going to vomit,
but I didn't. I smashed his head into the fender and caught his
hair in both my hands and kneed him in the nose. I'd never
done anything to him. We heard their car leave. I kissed her
and opened her blouse. I shot him and he fell. "You can get
me so damn hot," she said. Then I got myself some Coke out
of the icebox and mixed a drink. One was all I needed. She
told me how this man had three kids and a wife who didn't
like to dance. I didn't move. I could just touch her between
her legs and she'd be ready to come. I guess we were both
surprised. We were both quiet. "Let's get up and go home, and
we'll tell your mother first," I said. I didn't know whether to
just go on in or knock on the door. The one on Julie's side said
something to the one with the rifle. His pants were down around
his knees and she sounded like she was choking. "No," he said,
"I don't know you." It seemed that she was what I had been
wanting my whole life. I turned around and grabbed his head.
They didn't look like people who would raise a son like that.
"We've got a flat," he said, but the car looked level. The second
one went over to her. I didn't know what they were doing.

"Yes, you do," I said. Another, third boy stood in the rain with his hands in his pockets. I was lying on the ground in front of the car. Her body was the temple where I worshipped. They hit me in the head with the gun and then I couldn't see what they were doing with her. I blame that on him. He might have been their cousin. I'd seen his parents before. I eased through town. "Let's get married," I said. The rain was falling in front of the headlights. I had to pull over and stop. It was the best thing I'd ever done. I didn't have an inspection sticker and I was trying to stay away from the law. She'd never mentioned him. But they do. He'd been to the funeral of his brother. I didn't know what to do. "I'll do anything if you don't," she said. I thought she was full of bullshit. Sideways. I didn't like them anyway. I pulled the trigger. I saw then what they'd done. We pulled up into the graveyard and the tires slid in the mud. "He's got a gun," she said. I don't remember driving there. They were both naked and he was between her legs. He was dead, just like that. But the fetus was alive. We hadn't talked about telling anybody. I watched it, but I couldn't concentrate on it for thinking about what we were going to do later. She was still getting ready. He had it out and was holding it in his hand. There were a lot of things I could have said to him, I guess. She said she hoped it was a girl. I know I was scared. I cranked the car and let it warm up. The third one looked like he was puking in the ditch. It made a little red hole between his eyes. She had an abortion. What's bad is that he may be burning for an eternity because of me. She couldn't stop kissing me. I could remember, faintly, seeing them doing it when I was little.

When I grabbed the barrel, he turned loose and ran. When it was raining, it was wonderful to park with her. We'd have to get married soon. I know she was thinking about doing it just like me. I kicked the bottoms of his feet. But it's all posted now and you can't hunt on it. I helped her into the car and we looked for the third boy but we didn't see him. There was so much I had to tell her and so much I needed to tell her and in the end I told her nothing. And maybe we wouldn't even be able to make it. I couldn't feel her with one on. I took a shower and shaved, walking around naked in the house. I didn't want to see her hurt. She knew them. "Hey," I said. Jeans and a striped shirt. I didn't know what in the hell to do. I didn't mind killing him so much, after what he'd done. It was my child. I guess he was loosening the transmission bolts. So safe and warm. "Whenever you tell yours," I said. I turned on the defroster when it warmed up. I kept messing around with her. They used to come over and talk to her. The grass was high and there was an old dog pen or hog pen in the pasture with rotten posts and rusted wire. I'd always come right away the first time. We'd been going at each other for the last five months. He was crying and begging me not to do it. I begged him not to hurt her and he kicked me in the face. It hurt.

SAMARITANS

I was smoking my last cigarette in a bar one day, around the middle of the afternoon. I was drinking heavy, too, for several reasons. It was hot and bright outside, and cool and dark inside the bar, so that's one reason I was in there. But the main reason I was in there was because my wife had left me to go live with somebody else.

A kid came in there unexpectedly, a young, young kid. And of course that's not allowed. You can't have kids coming in bars. People won't put up with that. I was just on the verge of going out to my truck for another pack of smokes when he walked in. I don't remember who all was in there. Some old guys, I guess, and probably, some drunks. I know there was one old man, a golfer, who came in there every afternoon with shaky hands, drank exactly three draft beers, and told these crummy dirty jokes that would make you just close your eyes and shake your head without smiling if you weren't in a real good mood. And back then, I was never in much of a good mood. I knew they'd tell that kid to leave.

But I don't think anybody much wanted to. The kid didn't look good. I thought there was something wrong the minute he stepped in. He had these panicky eyes.

The bartender, Harry, was a big muscled-up guy with a beard. He was washing beer glasses at the time, and he looked up and saw him standing there. The only thing the kid had on was a pair of green gym shorts that were way too big for him. He looked like maybe he'd been walking down the side of a road for a long time, or something similar to that.

Harry, he raised up a little and said, "What you want, kid?" I could see that the kid had some change in his hand. He was standing on the rail and he had his elbows hooked over the bar to hold himself up.

I'm not trying to make this sound any worse than it was, but to me the kid just looked like maybe he hadn't always had enough to eat. He was two or three months overdue for a haircut, too.

"I need a pack a cigrets," he said. I looked at Harry to see what he'd say. He was already shaking his head.

"Can't sell em to you, son," he said. "Minor."

I thought the kid might give Harry some lip. He didn't. He said, "Oh," but he stayed where he was. He looked at me. I knew then that something was going on. But I tried not to think about it. I had troubles enough of my own.

Harry went back to washing his dishes, and I took another drink of my beer. I was trying to cut down, but it was so damn hot outside, and I had a bunch of self-pity loading up on me at that time. The way I had it figured, if I could just stay where I was until the sun went down, and then make my way home without getting thrown in jail, I'd be okay. I had some catfish I was going to thaw out later.

Nobody paid any attention to the kid after that. He wasn't making any noise, wasn't doing anything to cause people to look at him. He turned loose of the bar and stepped down off the rail, and I saw his head going along the far end toward the door.

But then he stuck his face back around the corner, and motioned me toward him with his finger. I didn't say a word, I just looked at him. I couldn't see anything but his eyes sticking up, and that one finger, crooked at me, moving.

I could have looked down at my beer and waited until he went away. I could have turned my back. I knew he couldn't stay in there with us. He wasn't old enough. You don't have to get yourself involved in things like that. But I had to go out for my cigarettes, eventually. Right past him.

I got up and went around there. He'd backed up into the dark part of the lounge.

"Mister," he said. "Will you loan me a dollar?"

He already had money for cigarettes. I knew somebody outside had sent him inside.

I said, "What do you need a dollar for?"

He kind of looked around and fidgeted his feet in the shadows while he thought of what he was going to say.

"I just need it," he said. "I need to git me somethin."

He looked pretty bad. I pulled out a dollar and gave it to him. He didn't say thanks or anything. He just turned and pushed open the door and went outside. I started not to follow him just then. But after a minute I did.

The way the bar's made, there's a little enclosed porch you come into before you get into the lounge. There's a glass door where you can stand inside and look outside. God, it was hot out there. There wasn't even a dog walking around. The sun was burning down on the parking lot, and the car the kid was crawling into was about what I'd expected. A junky-ass old Rambler, wrecked on the right front end, with the paint almost faded off, and slick tires, and a rag hanging out of the grill. It was parked beside my truck and it was full of people. It looked like about four kids in the backseat. The woman who was driving put her arm over the seat, said something to the kid, and then reached out and whacked the hell out of him.

I started to go back inside so I wouldn't risk getting involved. But Harry didn't have my brand and there was a pack on the dash. I could see them from where I was, sitting there in the sun, almost close enough for the woman to reach out and touch.

I'd run over a dog with my truck that morning and I wasn't feeling real good about it. The dog had actually been sleeping in the road. I thought he was already dead and was just going to straddle him until I got almost on top of him, when he raised up suddenly and saw me, and tried to run. Of course I didn't have time to stop by then. If he'd just stayed down, he'd have been all right. The muffler wouldn't have even hit him. It was just a small dog. But, boy, I heard it when it hit the bottom of my truck. It went *WHOP!* and the dog—it was a white dog—came rolling out from under my back bumper with all four legs stiff, yelping. White hair was flying everywhere. The air was full of it. I could see it in my rearview mirror. And I don't know why I was thinking about that dog I'd killed while I was watching those people, but I was. It didn't make me feel any better.

They were having some kind of terrible argument out there in that suffocating hot car. There were quilts and pillows piled up in there, like they'd been camping out. There was an old woman on the front seat with the woman driving, the one who'd whacked hell out of her kid for coming back empty-handed.

I thought maybe they'd leave if I waited for a while. I thought maybe they'd try to get their cigarettes somewhere else. And then I thought maybe their car wouldn't crank. Maybe, I thought, they're waiting for somebody to come along with some jumper cables and jump them off. But I didn't have any jumper cables. I pushed open the door and went down the steps.

There was about three feet of space between my truck and their car. They were all watching me. I went up to the window of my truck and got my cigarettes off the dash. The woman driving turned all the way around in the seat. You couldn't tell how old she was. She was one of those women that you can't tell about. But probably somewhere between thirty and fifty. She didn't have liver spots. I noticed that.

I couldn't see all of the old woman from where I was standing. I could just see her old wrinkled knees, and this dirty slip she had sticking out from under the edge of her housecoat. And her daughter—I knew that was who she was—didn't look much better. She had a couple of long black hairs growing out of this mole on her chin that was the size of a butter bean. Her hair kind of looked like a mophead after you've used it for a long time. One of the kids didn't even have any pants on.

She said, "Have they got some cold beer in yonder?" She shaded her eyes with one hand while she looked up at me.

I said, "Well, yeah. They do. But they won't sell cigarettes to a kid that little."

"It just depends on where they know ye or not," she said. "If they don't know ye then most times they won't sell em to you. Is that not right?"

I knew I was already into something. You can get into something like that before you know it. In a minute.

"I guess so," I said.

"Have you got—why you got some, ain't you? Can I git one of them off you?" She was pointing to the cigarettes in my hand. I opened the pack and gave her one. The kid leaned out and wanted to know if he could have one, too.

"Do you let him smoke?"

"Why, he just does like he wants to," she said. "Have you not got a light?"

The kid was looking at me. I had one of those Bics, a red one, and when I held it out to her smoke, she touched my hand for a second and held it steady with hers. She looked up at me and tried to smile. I knew I needed to get back inside right away, before it got any worse. I turned to go and what she came out with stopped me dead in my tracks.

"You wouldn't buy a lady a nice cold beer, would you?" she said. I turned around. There was this sudden silence, and I knew that everybody in the car was straining to hear what I would say. It was serious. Hot, too. I'd already had about five and I was feeling them a little in the heat. I took a step back without meaning to and she opened her door.

"I'll be back in a little bit, Mama," she said.

I looked at those kids. Their hair was ratty and their legs were skinny. It was so damn hot you couldn't stand to stay out in it. I said, "You gonna leave these kids out here in the sun?"

"Aw, they'll be all right," she said. But she looked around kind of uncertainly. I was watching those kids. They were as quiet as dead people.

I didn't want to buy her a beer. But I didn't want to make a big deal out of it, either. I didn't want to keep looking at those kids. I just wanted to be done with it.

"Lady," I said, "I'll buy you a beer. But those kids are burning up in that car. Why don't you move it around there in the shade?"

"Well." She hesitated. "I reckon I could," she said. She got back in and it cranked right up. The fan belt was squealing, and some smoke farted out from the back end. But she limped it around to the side and left it under a tree. Then we went inside together.

The first Bud she got didn't last two minutes. She sucked the can dry. She had on some kind of military pants and a man's long-sleeved work shirt, and house shoes. Blue ones, with a little fuzzy white ball on each. She had the longest toes I'd ever seen.

Finally I asked her if she wanted another beer. I knew she did.

"Lord yes. And I need some cigrets too if you don't care. Marlboro Lights. Not the menthol. Just reglar lights."

I didn't know what to say to her. I thought about telling her I was going to the bathroom, and then slipping out the door. But I really wasn't ready to leave just yet. I bought her another beer and got her some cigarettes.

"I'm plumb give out," she said. "Been drivin all day."

I didn't say anything. I didn't want anybody to think I was going with her.

"We tryin to git to Morgan City Loozeanner. M'husband's sposed to've got a job down there and we's agoin to him. But I don't know," she said. "That old car's about had it."

I looked around in the bar and looked at my face in the mirror behind the rows of bottles. The balls were clicking softly on the pool tables.

"We left from Tuscalooser Alabama," she said. "But them younguns has been yellin and fightin till they've give me a sick headache. It shore is nice to set down fer a minute. Ain't it good and cool in here?"

I watched her for a moment. She had her legs crossed on the bar stool and about two inches of ash hanging off her cigarette. I got up and went out the door, back to the little enclosed porch. By looking sideways I could see the Rambler parked under the shade. One of the kids was squatted down behind it, using the bathroom. I thought about things for a while and then went back in and sat down beside her.

"Ain't many men'll hep out a woman in trouble," she said. "Specially when she's got a buncha kids."

I ordered myself another beer. The old one was hot. I set it up on the bar and she said, "You not goin to drank that?"

"It's hot," I said.

"I'll drank it," she said, and she pulled it over next to her. I didn't want to look at her anymore. But she had her eyes locked on me and she wouldn't take them off. She put her hand on my wrist. Her fingers were cold.

"It's some people in this world has got thangs and some that ain't," she said. "My deddy used to have money. Owned three service stations and a sale barn. Had four people drove trucks fer him. But you can lose it easy as you git it. You ought to see him now. We cain't even afford to put him in a rest home."

I got up and went over to the jukebox and put two quarters in. I played some John Anderson and some Lynn Anderson and then I punched Narvel Felts. I didn't want to have to listen to what she had to say.

She was lighting a cigarette off the butt of another one when I sat down beside her again. She grabbed my hand as soon as it touched the bar.

"Listen," she said. "That's my mama out yonder in that car. She's seventy-eight year old and she ain't never knowed nothin but hard work. She ain't got a penny in this world. What good's it done her to work all her life?"

"Well," I said, "she's got some grandchildren. She's got them."

"Huh! I got a girl eighteen, was never in a bit a trouble her whole life. Just up and run off last year with a goddamn sand nigger. Now what about that?"

"I don't know," I said.

"I need another beer!" she said, and she popped her can down on the bar pretty hard. Everybody turned and looked at us. I nodded to Harry and he brought a cold one over. But he looked a little pissed.

"Let me tell you somethin," she said. "People don't give a shit if you ain't got a place to sleep ner nothin to eat. They don't care. That son of a bitch," she said. "He won't be there when we git there. If we ever git there." And she slammed her face down on the bar, and started crying, loud, holding onto both beers.

Everybody stopped what they were doing. The people shooting pool stopped. The guys on the shuffleboard machine just stopped and turned around.

"Get her out of here," Harry said. "Frank, you brought her in here, you get her out."

I got down off my stool and went around to the other side of her, and I took her arm.

"Come on," I said. "Let's go back outside."

I tugged on her arm. She raised her head and looked straight at Harry.

"*Fuck* you," she said. "You don't know nothin about me. You ain't fit to judge."

"Out," he said, and he pointed toward the door. "Frank," he said.

"Come on," I told her. "Let's go."

It hadn't cooled off any, but the sun was a little lower in the sky. Three of the kids were asleep in the backseat, their hair plastered to their heads with sweat. The old woman was sitting in the car with her feet in the parking lot, spitting brown juice out the open door. She didn't even turn her head when we walked back to the car. The woman had the rest of the beer in one hand, the pack of Marlboro Lights in the other. She leaned against the fender when we stopped.

"You think your car will make it?" I said. I was looking at the tires and thinking of the miles they had to go. She shook her head slowly and stared at me.

"I done changed my mind," she said. "I'm gonna stay here with you. I love you."

Her eyes were all teary and bitter, drunk-looking already, and I knew that she had been stomped on all her life, and had probably been forced to do no telling what. And I just shook my head.

"You can't do that," I said.

She looked at the motel across the street.

"Let's go over there and git us a room," she said. "I want to."

The kid who had come into the bar walked up out of the hot weeds and stood there looking at us for a minute. Then he got in the car. His grandmother had to pull up the front seat to let him in. She turned around and shut the door.

"I may just go to Texas," the woman said. "I got a sister lives out there. I may just drop these kids off with her for a while and go on out to California. To Los Vegas."

I started to tell her that Las Vegas was not in California, but it didn't matter. She turned the beer up and took a long drink of it, and I could see the muscles and cords in her throat pumping and working. She killed it. She dropped the can at her feet, and it hit with a tiny tinny sound and rolled under the car. She wiped her mouth with the back of her hand, tugging hard at her lips, and then she wiped her eyes.

"Don't nobody know what I been through," she said. She was looking at the ground. "Havin to live on food stamps and feed four younguns." She shook her head. "You cain't do it," she said. "You cain't hardly blame nobody for wantin to run off from it. If they was any way I could run off myself I would."

"That's bad," I said.

"That's terrible," I said.

She looked up and her eyes were hot.

"What do you care? All you goin to do is go right back in there and git drunk. You just like everybody else. You ain't never had to go in a grocery store and buy stuff with food stamps and have everbody look at you. You ain't never had to go hungry. Have you?"

I didn't answer.

"Have you?"

"No."

"All right, then," she said. She jerked her head toward the building. "Go on back in there and drank ye goddamn beer. We made it this far without you."

She turned her face to one side. I reached back for my wallet because I couldn't think of anything else to do. I couldn't stand to look at them anymore.

I pulled out thirty dollars and gave it to her. I knew that their troubles were more than she'd outlined, that they had awful things wrong with their lives that thirty dollars would never cure. But I don't know. You know how I felt? I felt like I feel when I see those commercials on TV, of all those people, women and kids, starving to death in Ethiopia and places, and I don't send money. I know that Jesus wants you to help feed the poor.

She looked at what was in her hand, and counted it, jerking the bills from one hand to the other, two tens and two fives. She folded it up and put it in her pocket, and leaned down and spoke to the old woman.

"Come on, Mama," she said. The old woman got out of the car in her housecoat and I saw then that they were both wearing exactly the same kind of house shoes. She shuffled around to the front of the car, and her daughter took her arm.

They went slowly across the parking lot, the old woman limping a little in the heat, and I watched them until they went up the steps that led to the lounge and disappeared inside. The kid leaned out the window and shook his head sadly. I pulled out a cigarette and he looked up at me.

"Boy you a dumb sumbitch," he said.

And in a way I had to agree with him.

NIGHT LIFE

I decided a long time ago that it isn't easy meeting them, not for me. Some guys can just walk up to a woman and start talking to her, start saying anything. I can't. I have to wait and work up my nerve, have a few beers. I have to sit at a table for a while, or the bar, and look them over and find the one who looks like she won't turn a man down. This sometimes means picking one who is sitting by herself, who is maybe a little older than most, maybe even one who doesn't look very good. Sometimes I wait until she dances with another man, then go over and make my move after she sits back down. Sometimes, if I see one whose looks I like, I send a drink over to her table. But it isn't easy meeting them.

I'm in a bar just outside the city limits Friday night when three women come in and take a table next to the dance floor, the last table not taken. I order another beer and look out over the crowd, the band playing, the couples who have found each other drifting over the floor like smoke. Some of the tables have three and four women, some have couples, some have men, and one table has a girl by herself. I check her out.

She has on a black dress and white stockings, is dressed, I think, a little like a witch. She has a bottle in a brown paper sack sitting on the table and she holds onto her solitary drink with both hands. She seems to have eyes for only this. I sip on my beer for a while and eye the creeping clock above the taps and finally I go over. She looks up and sees me coming her way and looks away.

"Hi," I say, when I stop beside her chair. I wish the band wouldn't play rock and roll; you can't even talk over the noise.

She smiles but she doesn't say anything. I'm going to be shot down.

I lean over and shout above the music: "How you doing?" She says something that I think is "okay" and I feel completely stupid, leaning over her like this. She looks like she just wants me to go away quickly and leave her alone. I won't score. She won't dance. Friday night is flying away.

"Want to dance?" I shout in her ear. The black horn player is crouched on the stage in front of the mike, the spotlight on him, his cheeks ballooned out as he blows and sweats, his jeweled fingers flying over the valves. She shakes her head and gives me a sad look. Smoke two feet thick hangs from the ceiling.

"Hell, come on," I say, putting on my friendliest smile, feeling my confidence—what little I had to start with—ebbing away. They're all like this. They won't talk to you, they won't dance. Why do they come out to a place like this if they don't want to meet men? "I'm not going to bite you," I say.

She takes one hand off her drink and leans slightly toward me. "Thanks anyway," she says. The flesh around her eyes looks dark, it's bruised, she's hurt. Maybe somebody slapped her. Maybe she said the wrong thing to the wrong man and he popped her. I know it can happen between a man and a woman. It can happen in a second.

"You live around here?" I say. I don't know what to say; I'm just saying anything to try and keep her talking.

She shakes her head, closes her eyes briefly. Patience. She's weary of this, maybe, these strange men asking, always asking, never stopping. "No. I live at Hattiesburg. I'm just up here for the weekend."

"You waiting on somebody?"

She draws back and blinks. Now she'll tell me it's none of my business. "Not really," she says. "I'm just waiting."

"Well come on and dance, then," I say.

She opens a small brown purse that looks like a dead mole and pulls out a white cigarette. I fish up my lighter and give her some fire. She inhales and coughs, her tiny fist balled at her mouth. Maybe she's had a bigger fist at her mouth. Maybe she likes it.

"Thanks," she says.

"You going to school at Hattiesburg?" I say.

She nods, looks around. "Yeah."

"Just up here living it up on the weekend."

"Not really. I just came up to Jackson to sort of be by myself for a while."

Something's bothering her, I can tell. She only wants to be left alone. She doesn't want to dance. She has her own bottle and her own table, her own troubles of which I know nothing. So I draw back a chair and put one foot up in it, rest my elbow on my knee. "How come?" I say.

She cups her face in her other hand and dabs at the ashtray with the cigarette.

"Oh. You know. Just getting away from everything."

"Yeah," I say. I know the feeling. I begin wishing I'd never walked over here. "What's your name?"

"Lorraine," this Lorraine says. She doesn't ask me my name.

"You look sad, Lorraine. What's wrong?"

"Nothing," she says, apparently only mildly pissed. "Nothing's wrong. I just want to be by myself for a while. I've just got some things I have to deal with."

I know. I know all people have things they must deal with. I have things I must deal with. I must deal with lonesome Friday nights, and these little semihostile confrontations sometimes occur as a result. But I don't know when to stop.

"Don't you like to dance?" I say. I feel like a fool. Am a fool.

"Sure. Sure I like to dance. I just don't feel like it tonight."

"Well," I say. I hate to get shot down, blown out of the saddle. But most of the time, I get shot down. I hate to have to turn away and go back to the bar without even a dance. I hate for them to beat me like this. But she probably does have some problem. There's probably a man involved somewhere, somehow. Possibly even a woman.

"Don't take it personally," she says. "Maybe some other night."

"Sure," I say, and I turn away. I walk a few steps and stop. I look back at her. She's taking the top off the bottle. I don't know what's the matter with me. I go back to her table.

"You sure you don't want to dance?" I say.

"No," she says, not even looking up. "Not now. Please leave me alone."

She's just lucky is all. She doesn't know just how damn lucky she is. The last of the Budweiser is almost warm, so I raise it aloft and signal to the sullen barmaid. I know her. She knows me. Her wet swollen hands reach into a dark cooler. I give her money but she doesn't speak. She doesn't want to look at me. Her heavy breasts sway as she rubs the bar hard, her eyes down. I watch them move. I watch her move away. She finds something to do at the other end of the bar. I take a drink.

A large number of people are wanting in the bathroom. I wait for three or four minutes before I can get inside the door, and then it's old piss, wet linoleum, knifecarvings above stained urinals that shredded butts have clogged. Water is weeping out from the partitioned commode stall where there is never any toilet paper. Others in line behind me are now waiting their turn. Their faces are scarred and murderous; it won't do to bump into them. To these no apology is acceptable. They'll cut their knuckles again and again on my broken teeth after I'm on the floor.

I go back out, into the noise and the smoke and the dark.

A woman touches my wrist when I go by her table, one of the three I saw earlier.

"Hey," she says. "How come you ain't asked me to dance yet?"

And there she is. Dark hair. Pale face. Sweater.

"I was fixing to," I say. "You want to wait till the band starts back up?"

"Set down," she says. She pulls out a chair and I sit.

"Where's your friends?" I say. I hope they won't come back. I don't know why she's picked me, but I'm glad somebody has. Even if the night turns out wasted there is hope at this moment.

"They over yonder," she points. "I've seen you before."

"In here?" I need my beer. "Let me go over here and get my beer and I'll be right back." She nods and smiles and I can't tell much about her except she's got knockers. I get my beer and come back.

"I saw you in here other night," she says. "Last weekend."

That's not right; I worked all weekend last weekend, trying to make more money. But I say, "Yeah. I come in here about every weekend."

Dark hair. Pale face. Sweater. Knockers. Jeans. I look down. Tennis shoes. With black socks.

"I used to come in here with my husband all the time," she says. "You want a drink?"

I lift my beer. We sit for a while without saying anything. The band is coming back, moving around on the stage and talking behind the dead mikes.

"That's a pretty good band," I say.

"Yeah. If you like nigger music. I wish they'd get a good country band. You like country music?"

"Yeah," I say. "Sure." But I wish I knew George Thorogood personally.

"Who you like?"

I have to think. "Aw. I like old Ricky Skaggs pretty good. Vern Gosden, I like him a lot. John Anderson."

"I used to be a singer," she says.

"Oh really?" I'm surprised. "Where?"

She looks around. She shrugs. I watch her breasts rise and fall. "Just around."

"I mean, professionally?" I sip my beer.

"Well. I sung at the Tupelo Mid-South Fair and Dairy Show in nineteen seventy-six. Had a three-piece band. That's where I met my husband."

"You're divorced," I say.

"Huh. Wish I was."

Here's the one thing I don't need: to get hooked up with somebody who has more problems than I do. I'm already on probation. I don't need to get hooked up with somebody who will sit here all night telling me how her husband fucked her over. But she has some really nice, truly wonderful breasts. It won't hurt to sit here and talk to her for a while. Maybe she's as lonely as I am.

"What? Are you separated?" I say.

"Yeah."

"How long?"

"About two weeks. Listen. I don't give a shit what he does. He's a sorry son of a bitch. I don't care if I don't never see him again."

"You're just out to have a good time."

"Damn right."

I tell her I think we can have one.

By ten we're out on the parking lot in her new Lincoln (surprise) and she's braced up against the driver's door. I have her sweater and bra all pushed up above her breasts and I'm moaning and kissing and trying to get her pants down. We're half hidden in the shadow of the building, but the neon lights are shining on the hood and part of the front seat. People in certain areas of the parking lot can see what we're doing. I don't care; I'm hot. Her nipples have been in and out of my mouth and she's halfway or halfheartedly trying to fight me off. She smells of talcum powder and light sweat. We've been kissing for ten minutes, but she doesn't seem to be excited. I know already, deep down, that something is wrong. She keeps looking out over the parking lot.

"Oh baby," I moan. I kiss the side of her neck and taste makeup on my tongue, slightly bitter. Patooey. "Let's do it," I say.

"Not here," she says. She pushes out from under me and takes both hands and tugs her bra and sweater back into place. I look at her for a moment and turn away. Not here. That might mean maybe somewhere else.

"Oh we'll *do* it," she says. Sure. "We just can't right now."

She rubs the side of my face. "My husband might be around here."

"Your husband?" I say. What's this? "I thought you said you weren't worried about him." It's always like this. They all have some problem they have to lay on you before they'll give it to you, and even then sometimes they won't give it to you. "What? You think he might come around here?"

She brushes the hair up away from her eyes and pulls at her pants. She pulls down one of the visor mirrors and checks her face.

"He might. I told you we used to come over here."

"You said you didn't give a shit what he did."

"I don't."

"Then what are you worried about?"

"I'm not worried. I just don't want him to catch me doing anything."

"Aw," I say. "Okay." I understand now. She's another one of the crazy ones. I don't know why I'm the one who always finds them, goes straight to them like a pointer after birds. They're not worth the trouble. They drive me nuts with their kids and their divorces and their diet pills and their friends in trouble and their ex-husbands for whom they still carry the torch. They promise and promise and promise. I know she's crazy now, I know the thing to do now is just forget about it, go back inside, leave her out here. "Well, I'm going back in here and get me a beer," I say. "I don't want to get mixed up with you and your husband. I'll see you later."

I slide over to the door—I don't have to slide far—and open

it. I step out onto the parking lot and look back in at her. She doesn't look up. She has some secret hurt in her heart that matters to her and doesn't matter to me. I think about this for a moment. I weigh various possibilities and things in my head. For a moment I'm tempted to get back in and talk to her. But then I shut the door and walk away.

They call me in from the car bay the next day and tell me I've got a phone call. I figure it's probably my mother wanting me to bring home something from the store, eggs or milk. I have grease all over my hands, under my fingernails, too, where it's always hard to get out, so I tear off a paper towel and pick up the extension with that.

"Hello," I say.

"Hey!"

I answer slowly. "Oh. Yeah." I recognize the voice.

"This is Connie. What you doing?"

"Well," I say, "right now I'm trying to fix a Buick. What can I do for you?" I look around and eye the shop foreman watching me. They don't pay me to talk on the phone unless I'm ordering parts.

"I just wanted to see what you's doing tonight. I wanted to talk to you about last night. Can you talk?"

I slip the receiver down between my head and my shoulder and wipe my hands with the paper towel. "Yeah," I say. "I guess I can for a minute. What's on your mind?"

"Well, I just wanted to tell you I was sorry about last night. About the way I acted. I'd been drinking before I ever got over there and we—Sheila and Bonita and me—we'd been talking about Roland and me before we ever come over there."

"Roland," I say. "Your husband."

"Right," she says, seems happy to say it. "We been married eight years. We got two kids. You know the kids is the ones always suffers in something like this."

"Yeah," I say. Well, sure. Sure they do. "I guess so," I say.

"I'm at home and I was thinking about last night. I mean, when we was out in the car and all. I was just upset. I didn't mean to act like that."

She's talking like she did something wrong. But all she did was refuse to take her pants off. In a public parking lot. Where anybody could have walked up to the car and looked in, seen her in all her naked glory for free. I'm uneasy remembering this, my half-drunk horny stupidity. I could have gone too far. I'm not supposed to be in bars anyway.

"Well," I say. "Hell. You don't owe me any apology or anything. I mean. We just met. You know. Out in the car and all. . . . you don't have to explain anything to me."

"I feel like I ought to, though," she says. "I was just wondering what you were gonna do tonight. I thought I'd see if you wanted to get a drink somewhere. If you're not busy." She lowers her voice. "I mean I liked it. In the car."

I know now that I shouldn't have tried that anyway. She just had me so turned on. . . .

I say, "You did, huh?" I'm seeing it again now, how the light played over her breasts, how they looked when I pushed her bra up.

"Well," I say, "I don't have anything planned."

"Okay," she says. She sounds glad she called. "You want to meet me somewhere?"

"Sure," I say. "I guess so. Hell, we can drink a beer or something."

"I'd really like to tell you why I acted the way I did last night, Jerry."

"It's Gary."

"Right. Gary. I knew it was Gary. You want to go back out there? Where we were last night?"

I start to say no, let's go someplace else, but she says, quickly, "It's close to my house and all. I'll have to get somebody to keep my kids and they know the number there if anything happens."

"Okay," I say. "Listen. I've got a lot of work to do, so it may be late when I get off. Maybe around six or seven. I get all the overtime I can. Why don't we try to get out there about nine? That'll give me time to get home and get cleaned up and all. I've got to catch a ride."

"That's fine," she says. "I'll get us a table."

"Okay," I say. I think for a moment. I might as well go ahead and ask her. "Listen. You want me to get us a room?"

She waits three seconds before she answers. "Well. You can get one if you want to, Gary. I'm not promising anything. But you can get us a room if you want to."

She's already happy and high when I slide into a chair beside her. It looks like the only seat left in the place is the one she's been saving for me.

"Hey," I say, and I set a fifth on the table. She leans over and kisses me. Her eyes are bright even in the darkness; they seem to belong to a woman different somehow from the one I wrestled with in the car the night before. The table is no bigger than a car tire. "How long you been here?" I say.

On the floor to the music she moves with drunken feet, pressing herself against me, her washed hair in my face sweet and soft. We dance a few times and then she tells me she wants to talk.

"What it is, see, he's wanting to catch me. Messing around."

"I don't get it," I say. "How come?"

"He wants me to give him a divorce. But I ain't gonna do it. I ain't gonna do one thing that'll make him happy."

I don't care about any of this. I don't want to know her problems. She acts like she's the only one who has any.

"Let's talk about something besides you and your husband," I say. "Why don't you quit thinking about him? You'd probably have a better time. You know it?"

She seems to realize with sadness that what I'm saying is true. "I know it," she says. "I'll hush about him."

But she doesn't. She keeps bringing his name up and looking all around in the bar, trying to spot him at large. I know there is nothing to do but be patient. I have a motel key in my pocket.

We pull into a parking space next to the wall of a Day's Inn and she turns off the lights and ignition. The aluminum numerals on the red metal door read 214.

"Let's go in," I say. I open my door.

She turns her face away from me and stares at something across the parking lot. She's very quiet. Unhappy. Almost angry.

"What are you looking at?" I say. I see the back of her dark head move.

"Nothing." She pulls the keys out and opens the door. "Let's go on in. Now that you've got me out here we might as well."

I haven't twisted her arm to get her out here. She's driven us over here willingly. Now I don't know what's wrong with her. She gets out and comes around to the front of the car looking down, not looking at me. I slip the key in and unlock the door. I turn on the light. A motel room like any other. I set what's left of the fifth on the plastic woodgrain table and go back and lean against the door. She is standing below the sidewalk, hugging herself with her arms, facing away. She seems to be looking at a blue Chevy pickup parked across the lot.

"You coming in?" I say.

Without answering she turns and comes by me and goes to sit on the bed. I shut the door and bolt it. I'm a little drunk. She'd better be careful. I take the bottle out of the sack and open it, tilt a burning drink down my throat. I hold it out to her.

"You want a drink?"

She shakes her head violently and stares at the floor.

"Well," I say. I look around and see the TV. "You want to watch some TV?"

"It doesn't matter," she says. "Nothing matters."

"Boy ain't we having just loads of fun," I say.

I turn on the TV and kick off my shoes and stretch out on the bed beside her, turning one of the pillows around so I can prop my head against it. I find an ashtray and move it over beside me. I sip from the bottle and wish I had some Coke. CNN news is on. After a while she turns around and lies down beside me. She doesn't say anything.

"You didn't have to come over here, you know," I say.

"I know," she says.

I don't know why I always have to pick some crazy woman. I used to be under the impression that after a man has put up with one of them, that that will do it for the rest of his life, that the others will all be halfway normal.

"You want to go back?" I ask her.

I turn just my head and watch her. She's lying on her side with her legs drawn up. She's wearing light blue slacks and a black top with red flowers.

"No," she says. "I want to stay here with you."

"Oh yeah?" I say. "Damn if you act like it."

For answer she reaches out and takes my hand and puts it on her breast. She rubs the hand over it for a moment and then slips it inside her blouse. I lean over and kiss her and push my fingers down into the cup of her bra. She slides a hand up my leg and I break away long enough to set the whiskey on the table, then roll on top of her.

"Cut the light out," she says.

"What?"

"Cut the light out."

I get up and pull off my shirt and flick off the light and we are left in the blue glow from the TV. Some massacre in a foreign country is being documented on the television screen: swollen bodies, murdered livestock in the streets. Black blood-stains on shattered brick walls. I push her shirt up and reach behind her and unsnap her bra, the heavy round meat easing into my hands. I kiss at her with an urgency she doesn't seem to share. I rub at the waistband of her pants and run my hands all over her. But there is no feeling in her kisses. She's tense. I twist her thick nipples between my fingers and after five min-utes I quit. She has worked her way upright in the bed and she sits now with her nice knockers poking out from underneath the twisted entanglements of her shirt and bra, looking not at me or the TV or her clothes but the wall.

I sit up and swing my legs to the floor and find my ciga-rettes. I light one and get my shirt off the floor.

"You ready to run me back to the club?" I say. "There's no need in us staying over here." Something is wrong with her. She doesn't even get excited. It's no wonder her husband has left her. She's cold as a fish.

"That's his pickup," she says.

"What?"

"That's Roland's pickup outside. He's got some woman over here. In one of these rooms." She looks at me. "Maybe right next to us."

I hate myself for being this way. For being so desperate. I already knew how it was going to turn out. I knew it would be exactly like this.

"Well, so what?" I say. "If he's screwing around on you, what are you so worried about?"

"I'm not worried," she says.

"The hell you ain't." I stand up and pull on my shirt. I know I need to get myself out of this room and away from her. It's not too late to go back to the bar and try to meet somebody else. Anybody will be better than her. Even the fat ones will be better than her. At least I can have a good time with them. They don't have problems. They don't waste the nights. "You're afraid he'll see you with me," I say.

"Would you just listen for one minute?" she says. "I been married to him since I was sixteen. We got some rental property we own together. He's a contractor. He didn't leave me. I left him! You don't understand."

"Yeah," I say. "I understand. I understand all of it. You're wanting somebody to listen to all your problems and I ain't no fucking head doctor. Just take me back to the club or let me out somewhere and I'll catch a ride home. Hell, it's Saturday night. I got to go back to work Monday. You know what I'm saying?"

She fastens her bra back together and pulls her shirt down. By the time I get out the door to the running car, I'm surprised she hasn't left me. The truck we saw earlier is gone, but she doesn't mention it. I get in with her and sit close to the door all the way back. I look at her breasts. They are magnificent. I want to suggest another scenario, but I don't.

I'm living with my mother again and Sunday is a chicken dinner, just the two of us. Mashed potatoes and English peas, gravy. I sleep late on Sunday, then go down to the road and pick up the papers, the *Commercial Appeal* from Memphis and the *Clarion-Ledger* from Jackson. The rest of my morning is taken up with reading these papers, especially the movie and book pages, and drinking coffee and smoking cigarettes until my mother comes in from church and calls me to dinner. I don't have a car now; a lawyer has the money it brought, so now I read the pages with the car ads, too. I want to buy a new one, have been toying with the idea, and try to save my money for that.

Sunday afternoon, I'm asleep in the bed that held me as a child when the phone rings. I wake and turn and hear my mother moving toward me in the empty house, her feet and weight ponderous on the old boards, hesitant. She's coming to see if I'm asleep and she probably hopes I am. She opens the door and sees me. She says there is some woman who wants to talk to me. I know somehow, freshly awake from dreams of erotica and hanging breasts, deliciously rested, ready for the last night of the weekend. I get up and go to the kitchen and shut the door. It's her.

"Gary?" she says.

"Yeah."

"It's Connie."

"Yeah. I know." What does she want and why has she picked me? Why can't she see that I'm bad for her? That I can't take much more?

"Did I wake you up?"

"Yeah, matter of fact you did."

"Aw, I'm sorry. I didn't mean to wake you up. I guess I shoulda called later. I didn't mean to wake you up."

"Listen," I say. "What do you want?" There's no need to be nice to her anymore. I'm through with her, I don't want her to start calling over here and bothering my mother when I'm not home. I don't even want her calling over here. My mother asks too many questions as it is. Any man twenty-eight years old ought to be able to come and go without his mother asking him where he's going every time.

"I just wanted to talk," she says, and she says that in a pleading voice. "Can you talk?" Suddenly she sounds cheerful and sober.

"I don't know," I say. "I mean, I don't see much point in it. I don't even know what you want. I don't think you know what you want." I can't see my cigarettes. "Hold on," I say. "I've got to find a cigarette."

I don't wait for her to answer. I go into the living room and get my pack and my lighter. I light one and look out the window at the passing cars, the uncut grass. My mother watches from behind her eyeglasses where she sits with the Bible of God cupped in her lap. She says nothing, but I see the fear she has. After a while I go back and pick up the telephone again. "All right," I say, making the weariness in my voice plain.

It's kind of hard, not having a car. I have to be careful to get with somebody who has wheels. I have to make sure of that early on. I don't mind paying for a room if the woman doesn't mind us going in her car. It complicates things, makes them more difficult. But I can't take them home, not while I'm living with my mother. She wouldn't allow it. I know what would happen if I tried it. I've imagined it before, and it isn't nice. It's awful. Doors jerked open and covers grabbed.

"Listen," she says. "I know I acted terrible last night. It was just his truck over there that did it. You got to understand, Gary, we been married ten years. You just don't throw ten years away without thinking about it."

"Right," I say. First eight years, now ten years. I must deal with her, get rid of her. "But it ain't none of my business. Let me explain something to you. When I go out on the weekend, all I'm looking for is to have a good time. All right? I mean I don't think I have to go to bed with every girl I meet. I've been married. Not as long as you, but I've been married. I know what it's like." I'm not saying what I mean to say. "You just act too damn strange for me, okay? You get depressed, and I don't need to be around somebody that's depressed all the time. It gets me depressed, too. Now that's all it is. If you still love your husband, fine. You need to try to work everything out with him. That's between you and him. I don't have anything to do with it. I just don't want you to call me anymore."

That should do it. That should make her mad enough to where she'll say something, then hang up on me. She doesn't.

"Oh, Gary. Don't be mad. I've been thinking over everything today. Listen. I called my husband and you know what I told him?"

"What?" I don't want to hear this shit.

"I told him I wanted a divorce. I told him I was going to try to get eight hundred dollars a month out of him. He started talking sweet then. He wants us to get back together now. What you think about that?"

"I don't know," I say. "I don't care," I say. I open the icebox and find a beer. Then I look a little longer and find the schnapps.

"I told him I saw him last night. At that motel. But anyway, that ain't what I called you about. I called you about something else."

"What?"

"I got us a room tonight. Just you and me. At the Holiday Inn. I already got it. I got the key right here."

I don't really believe that. "I don't really believe that," I say.

"Listen, Gary. I know I ain't acted right. I don't blame you for being disgusted with me. But it was just all that stuff with my ex. He's been going out on me for the longest. Friday night was the first time I'd ever been out without him. In ten years. Honest."

"Is that right?" I say. She's probably lying. She's probably just telling me all this so she can get me off again and drive me some more nuts telling me some more about it.

"I swear. Gary, I swear to God. May God strike me dead if I ain't telling the truth."

"Well," I say. I take a drink of my beer. Maybe she is telling the truth. Maybe they've had what she thought was a good marriage. It's happened before. You can go along fine for years and it can fall apart in a second. You can do things to each other that can never be forgiven. One word can lead to another word. You can lose control and a whole lot more. They can make you pay for one second of anger. They can make you pay with your house, and your car, and your money and self-respect. She doesn't have to tell me about marriage. I know already. Marriage is having to live with a woman. That's what marriage is.

But I won't have to see her after tonight. I won't put up with any more shit from her. I don't have to. I'm not married anymore. I won't be again.

"How's that sound?" she says.

"I guess it sounds all right," I say.

"Listen, baby, I'm gonna make up for everything tonight. I mean, everything."

"Well, okay," I say. She's convinced me. There's only one thing. I don't want her to pick me up here, at my mother's. "Where do you live?"

"I can come get you," she says.

"No. I'd rather you wouldn't," I say. "Listen. I've got a friend who'll give me a ride out to your house. You staying in the house?"

"Hell yes," she says. "I'm not gonna give it to my ex."

"I'll just get somebody to carry me out there, then. Where do you live?"

She tells me. I say I'll be there by seven. I feel a lot better about everything when I hang up the phone.

"You sure this is it?" I say to my friend.

The boy I'm riding with looks at the mailbox.

"That's the number. One hundred Willow Lane. Hell, Gary, there ain't nothing but rich people live up in here."

"Well damn," I say. "This is the address she gave me."

"Well, this is it then," my friend says. "You want me to wait on you?"

"I don't know. You might ought to."

"We'll just pull up in here and see if this is it."

We drive up a blacktopped lane to a house designed like a Swiss chalet. I guess that it's over four thousand square feet under this roof. It has big dormers and split shingles and massive columns of rough wood on the porch. There is a pool full of blue water in the backyard. The Lincoln I've been riding in and nuzzling her knockers in is parked in the drive.

"Hell. That's her car," I say. "I guess this is it."

She comes to the kitchen window and pushes the curtains aside.

"This is it," I say, when I see her. "I just didn't know it was this fancy."

"You better hang onto her," my friend says.

"Yeah. Maybe so. Well, thanks for the ride, Bobby. Let me give you some on the gas."

"Get outa here," he says.

I start pulling five dollars out of my billfold, but my friend leans across me and opens the door. "Get your butt outa here," he says. "Put that money back up."

"Hell, Bobby," I say. "It's a long way out here."

"I may need a ride from you sometime."

"You better take it."

"Go on. I'll see you later."

I get out, sticking the money back in my billfold, waving to my friend backing out of the driveway. The headlights retreat, swords of light through the motes of dust that hang and fall until he swings out and grabs low and peels away with a faint stench and high squeal of rubber. I listen to him hit the gears, to the little barks of rubber until he is gone. For a moment I wonder what I'm doing here. On another man's concrete. Another man's ride. Everything about this house is elegant. It's hard to believe this woman comes out of this place. But there she is, opening the door. I go up to her. She kisses me.

"Come on in," she says.

It's a dream room. High, vaulted ceilings, enclosed beams. Rams, bucks, bear heads mounted over the fireplace, and it of massive river stones. Carpet that covers my toes. I don't know what to say. I know now she wasn't lying about the contractor and the real estate. Or the kids. Two beautiful little girls are seated on the thick carpet in their nightgowns, one about two, the other about four. Dark hair like her, shy smiles.

"Hi," I say. They look up at me, smile, look down. They have toys, trucks, Sylvester the Cat on the floor. The remnants of their suppers are on paper plates beside them. Potato chips. Gnawed hamburger buns. They whisper things to each other and cast quick glances at me while they pretend not to watch.

"I'll be ready in just a minute, Gary," she says.

I look around. "Yeah. Okay," I say. I'm watching the little girls. They've taken my interest. They're so precious. I know they cannot comprehend what has happened to their daddy. I feel myself to be an intruder in this house, a homewrecker. The husband, the father, could come home and kill me this minute with a shotgun. Nothing would be said. No jury would convict the man. I don't belong here.

She has gone somewhere. I sit on the couch. The girls play with their trucks and croon softly to each other little songs without words, melodies made up in their own fantastic little minds. They move smooth as eels, boneless, their little arms and legs dimpled with fat.

"I'm ready," she says. I look around. She has her purse. She seems brisk, efficient. She has her keys. It's like she's suddenly decided to stop slumming. She has on trim black slacks, gold toeless shoes with low heels, a short mink jacket. Diamonds glitter in the lobes of her ears. Her breasts hang heavy and full in the lowcut shirt, and I know that tonight she will deny me nothing. She's smiling. She takes my arm as I stand up and she kisses me again. The children watch this puzzle in soundless wonder, this strange man kissing Mommy.

"Okay, girls, we'll be back after while," she says. They don't look up, don't appear to hear. "Sherry?" she says. "We're gone." She must be talking to somebody else in the house, somebody I can't see, the babysitter, I guess. "Sherry?" she says. "Did you hear me?"

"Let's go," she says to me, and she starts toward the door. She's searching for a key on her key ring.

"Bye, girls," I say. The oldest one gives me a solemn look, a dignified nod.

"Stay in here, now," she says. "Don't mess with the stove." We're halfway out the door when it hits me.

"Wait a minute," I say. She's locking the door, locking the

children into the house. I hear the lock click. "Where's your babysitter?"

"They're all right," she says. "We won't be gone long anyway. Not over a few hours."

"*Wait* a minute," I say. "You gonna leave them alone? Here?"

I've got my hand on her arm, I'm turning her to look at me in the lighted carport. She looks down at my hand and then up at me, surprised. She steps away.

"Well, it's not gonna hurt anything. They'll be all right."

"All right?" I say. "They're just little kids. I thought you said you had a babysitter."

"I couldn't get one," she says. "Now come on. Let's go. They've stayed by themselves before." She's going toward the car. I stand watching her dumbly, like a dumbass, like the dumbass I am.

"What if something happens, though?" I say. "What if the fucking house was to catch on fire?"

She stops and looks back. She holds her face up slightly, puts one hand on her hip. "Do you want to go or not?" she says.

"You told me last night the babysitter had your number so she could get ahold of you," I say. Then I realize. She's never had a babysitter. They've been locked up in this house the whole weekend, these children.

"Do you want to go or not?" she says.

I look through the curtains on the door. The girls have been watching it, but now they look back down at their toys. The youngest one gets up and walks away, out of sight. The oldest rolls her truck. I look at the woman standing by the door of a new Lincoln, waiting to carry me to a Holiday Inn. She's ready now, finally. And so am I.

"Come here," I say.

"What?"

"I said come here."

"Why? Get in, let's go."

I go around the hood after her, slowly. Her face changes.

"What is it?" she says. "What's wrong with you?"

"Come here," I say, and I know my face has changed, too.

"Hey," she says. "I don't know what you think you're doing."

I know what I'm doing. I have my hands on her now, and she can't pull away. She probably thinks I'm going to kill her, but I'm not. I'm going to keep my hands open this time, and not use my fists. I don't want to scare the little girls with blood. They would be frightened, and might remember it for the rest of their lives.

LEAVING TOWN

Her name was Myra and I could smell whiskey on her breath. She was nervous, but these days, you don't know who to let in your house. She'd seen my ad in the paper, she said, and wanted some new doors hung. We talked on the porch for a while and then she let me in.

It looked like she didn't have anything to do but keep her house clean. She gnawed her fingernails the whole time I was figuring the estimate. She kept opening and closing the top of her robe, like a nervous habit. Both the doors had been kicked out of their locks. The wood was splintered. She needed two new doors, some trim. Maybe two new locks. She wanted new linoleum in her dining room. I gave her a price for the labor and went on home, but I didn't think I'd get the job.

He was a polite young man. His name was Richard. He seemed to be very understanding when I explained that Harold had kicked the doors in. Of course I didn't tell him everything. All I wanted was to forget about Harold, and every time I looked at the doors I thought about him.

I tried to talk to him a little. I told him that I was divorced now and that it was a lot different when you're used to two salaries and then have to live on just one. I told him I didn't want to pay a whole lot for the work. He said the doors would run about forty dollars apiece. I had no idea they would be that high.

He had very nice-looking hands. They looked like strong hands, but gentle. I doubted if they'd ever been used to slap somebody, or to break down a door.

He didn't talk much. He was one of those quiet people who intrigue you because they keep so much inside. Maybe he was just shy. I thought the price he gave me was twenty or thirty dollars too high. I told him I'd think about it. But I needed the work done.

After he left, I fixed myself another drink and looked at the doors. They were those hollow-core things, they wouldn't keep out anybody who wanted in bad enough. I kept thinking about Richard. I wondered what it would be like to kiss him. I could imagine how it would be. How warm his hands would be. My life is halfway or more than halfway over. There's not much time left for things like that. I don't know why I even thought about it. He had the bluest eyes and they looked so sad. Maybe that was the reason. Whatever it was, I decided to call him back and let him do the work. I couldn't stand to look at those doors any longer.

I was feeding Tracey when she called. Betty was reading one of her police detective magazines. The phone rang three or four times. Betty acted like she didn't hear it. I got up with Tracey and went and answered it.

I was surprised that she called back. She'd already talked like I was too high. But people don't know what carpentry work is worth. You have to have a thousand dollars' worth of tools to even start.

She sounded like she was a little drunk. I guess she was lonely. When I was over there, she'd look at the doors and just shake her head. But I'd given her a reasonable price. It was cheaper than anybody else would have done it for. I didn't tell her that. She wouldn't have believed it.

I told her I could start the next night. She hadn't understood that I was going to do it at night. I had told her, though. She just hadn't been listening. She said she thought I was in business for myself. I told her I was, at night. I told her I had to work my other job in the daytime. Then she wanted to know all about that. She just wanted somebody to talk to. Tracey was going to sleep in my lap. I asked Betty if she'd take her but she wouldn't even look up. She was still reading her magazine.

She wanted to know didn't I get tired of working all the time, at night and on weekends. Hell, who wouldn't? I told her, sure, I got tired of it, but I needed the money. That was all I told her then. I didn't want to tell her about Tracey. I didn't want to tell her all my personal business.

She sat there for a while and didn't say anything. Then she wanted to know if there was any way I could come down on the price. That pissed me off. She wanted to know if that was the very least I could do it for. At first I told her I didn't see any way I could, but I needed the money. Hell, I have to put gas in my truck and all. . . .

I told her I'd cut it twenty more dollars but that was it. I told her if she couldn't live with that, she'd just have to find some-body else to do it. And I told her that if she found somebody cheaper, she wouldn't be satisfied with it.

I had to tell her a couple of times that I'd be there the next night. I told her I had to go by the building supply and get the doors. She wanted to talk some more, but I told her I had to put my baby to bed. Finally I got away from her. I wasn't really looking forward to going back.

I got up with Tracey and Betty wanted to know who that was on the phone. I told her a lady I was going to do some work for. Then she wanted to know what kind of work and how old a lady and was she married or divorced and what did she look like. I told her, Hell, normal, I guess, to let me put Tracey to bed.

She started crying when I laid her down and I had to stay in there with her and pet her a while. I guess her legs hurt. She finally went to sleep. Betty won't even get up with her at night. I have to. It doesn't matter if I've worked twelve hours or fourteen hours. She can't even hear an alarm clock. You can let one go off and hold it right in her ear. She won't even move.

She was smoking the last cigarette I had when I went back

in the living room. She said that kid hated her and I told her she just didn't have any patience with her. I picked up the empty pack and asked her if she had any more. She said she was out. I just looked at her. She'll sit in the house all day long and won't walk a half block to the store and get some, then smoke mine until she makes me run out. Then I have to go.

I got my jacket and told her I guessed I'd have to go get some. She told me to bring her some beer back. I told her I didn't have enough money to buy any beer. I wanted some too but I was almost broke. She told me to just write a check. She says that shit all the time. I told her we had enough to pay that doctor bill and that was it. Then she said something about the saw I bought. It was eighty-nine dollars. But good saws cost good money. And if I don't have a saw, I don't have a job.

She wanted to know when I was going to marry her. I told her I didn't know.

I went by the building supply the next day, after I got off from work. I priced the locks, but they were almost twenty dollars apiece. I decided to see if I could use the old locks on her doors and save her that much anyway. I signed for the doors and the trim, the linoleum.

I didn't want to go straight over there. I wanted to go home for a few minutes and see Tracey and get Betty to fix me something to eat. I'd asked Leon to let me borrow ten dollars until Friday, so I stopped at the store and got a six-pack of beer. You can't just go through life doing without everything.

I loaded up my sawhorses and left the linoleum in the carport. Tracey was sitting on the floor, wanting me to pick her up. I set the sack on the table and told Betty I'd brought her some beer. She was reading another magazine so I played with Tracey for a while. Then I got her building blocks and set her down with them and got one of the beers out of the sack. Dirty clothes were piled up everywhere. She won't wash until we don't have anything to wear. I lit a cigarette and just watched her. She didn't know I was in the room. I drank about half my beer. I had a lot of shit going through my head.

Finally I asked her if she could fix me something to eat before I went over there. I told her it would probably be late when I got back. I told her I was hungry.

She asked me what I wanted. I told her I didn't care, a sandwich, anything. She said she didn't know of anything we had to eat. She said I could go in there and look.

I told her I wanted some supper. She didn't look back up, and I thought, Work your ass off all day and come home and have to put up with some shit like this.

I sat there a while and then I got up and made out like I was going to the kitchen. She wasn't watching me anyway. She had her magazine up in front of her face, picking at the buttons on her blouse. I bent down behind the couch. I peeked over her shoulder to see what she was reading. THE LAUNDROMAT AXE MURDERER WOULDN'T COME CLEAN. I don't know how she can stand to read that shit. She gets so deep into it, she'll get her nails in her mouth. I got up on my knees right behind her. She was nibbling her bottom lip. I was just trying to have a little fun.

She jumped about two feet high when I went boo in her

ear. Turned around and slammed her magazine down. She was pissed. Bad pissed.

I told her I was just playing with her. She told me to just go on and leave. Said I was always hollering about saving money. Why didn't I go out and make some? Instead of worrying the hell out of her?

I got up in her face, said let me tell you one goddamn thing. You lay around here on your ass all day long and don't do nothing. Won't clean the house up. Won't even wash Tracey's face. I told her if I could go out and work at night, she could fix me something to eat.

She said there wasn't anything to eat.

I said by God she could buy something.

She said give her some money and she might.

I told her I gave her money, and she spent it on those stupid fucking magazines.

She whispered to me. Hateful. If I was so damn unhappy then why didn't I just leave? Just pack up and go right now?

I didn't answer. I picked up Tracey and she put her arms around my neck. We went into the kitchen. I looked in the refrigerator. There was some old bacon, and a half cup of chili in a Tupperware bowl, and a quart of milk, and a little brown hamburger meat, and one hot dog. I found some Rice Krispies under the counter. I fixed two bowls and ate with Tracey. I washed her hands and her face.

I didn't want to leave. I'd said some of the words I'd been wanting to say but I hadn't said all of them. My words wouldn't hurt her as bad as hers hurt me. I held onto Tracey and looked at my watch. There wasn't much time. Your life goes by and if you spend it unhappy, what's the point? If staying won't make you happy, and leaving ruins somebody else's life, what's the answer?

I didn't know. I still don't. But I'd told her I'd be there by six. And finally I couldn't wait in the kitchen any longer.

I was so nervous I changed clothes three times before he got there. I ended up wearing a dress that was too short. I cleaned the house twice, even though I knew there would be sawdust and tools on the floor. I'd been thinking about him all day, I couldn't help it. He was so quiet and mysterious and he had such lovely hands. I'd had a few drinks, and I was going to offer him a drink when he got there. Just thinking about him being all alone in the house with me excited me. Maybe if he had a few drinks, he'd loosen up and talk to me. I wanted to talk to somebody so badly. It's not easy being alone after being married for thirty years. It's not easy to come home to a house so quiet you can hear a clock ticking.

I kept waiting and looking at my watch, and I kept drinking. I thought it would calm me down. I was so nervous my hands were just trembling.

Finally he pulled up and I looked out through the curtain in the living room. He had two doors and two sawhorses in the back of his pickup. I watched him get out and put on a tool belt and lift the doors from the truck.

I opened the door for him and smiled and told him he was right on time. He said hi or something, and then started bringing everything in. He didn't have much to say. I just watched him and smiled. He brought in some kind of a crowbar and a power saw and a long orange extension cord. I couldn't get that idiotic grin off my face. I had a drink in one hand and a cigarette in the other. Harold used to tell me that if I didn't drink myself to death, I'd smoke myself to death. But he was always so cruel. Always so cruel.

I asked him if he would like a drink. He said he didn't like whiskey, and took the crowbar and tore the facing off the wall like he was mad at it. It made this awful screeching sound when the nails pulled loose. He just . . . attacked it. Within five minutes he had the frame and the door lying in the carport and was pulling finishing nails from the studs. The nails screamed when he pulled them. I said something about how he didn't waste any time. I was smiling. He said he wasn't making much money on this and had to get through as quick as he could.

I thought he was probably mad at me for talking him into coming down twenty dollars. But I'm single, I don't have Harold's money, I have to get by, too.

I told him I had some beer if he wanted one. He said let him get this door up and he might take one. He pulled a screwdriver out of his tool belt and stepped outside to the carport and closed the door behind him. Almost like he didn't have time to talk to me. Or was angry with me. I hadn't done anything to him. The paneling was rough and splintered where he'd taken the door off. You could see the wires inside the studs. You could see the nails. It all looked so raw.

I made myself another drink, and checked my makeup in

the hall mirror. You would have thought I was having a cocktail party the way I was acting. He was out in the carport and I watched him through the window. He was kneeling beside the door, doing something, I couldn't tell what. His shirt had come up and I could see the bumps of bone in his back. His back looked so smooth. I wanted to feel it with my hands, run my hands over it, up his ribs, down over his hips, I wanted him to put his mouth on my throat and slide it down to my breasts and take one of my nipples in his lips and say Myra, Myra. . . .

My goddamn back was killing me. If I bend over for more than five minutes at a time I can't straighten up. Sometimes in the mornings it hurts so bad I can just barely get out of bed. I have to get up and walk around and bend and stretch to get to where I can go to work. It usually stops hurting midway through the morning and starts hurting twice as bad around three. I'd been laboring for a bricklayer all that day, mixing his mortar and handing him his blocks. They just scab us out to whoever needs help on a big job. If you're not in the union you don't have any say. I can't stand the dues so I pay my own. But I'm afraid I'll get disabled. I'm afraid I won't be able to work anymore. I worry about that every day.

I fell three months ago. We were bricking a bank. A scaffold leg collapsed, one of those cheap ones they rent from the building supply. I was fourteen feet up, not that high, but I landed on a sheet of plywood that was propped up against a water cooler. I thought I'd broken my back. Everybody who saw me fall thought I'd broken my back. When the ambulance came for me, they treated me like a patient with a broken back. They pulled traction on me and immobilized me. I was screaming. I bit my tongue.

My foreman came to see me in the hospital. He told me the company took care of its employees. He only stayed a few minutes. I could tell he couldn't wait to get out of there.

I had to go on workmen's comp after I got out of the hospital. What I drew was about half my pay. You can't live on half money. You've got to have whole money. I went over to the job a few times, to talk to the guys I worked with, but I was just in the way. They couldn't work and talk to me, too. I stopped going after a while. I stayed home and drank beer with Betty and read those Little Golden Books to Tracey.

I'd never felt so useless in my whole life. There wasn't anything to occupy me. Betty didn't want to do it. I had to do the grocery shopping to make our money stretch. We fought over the money, over the TV, over anything and everything. I had to put up with these assholes every week in the office where I got my check. Some days I wanted to just go away somewhere and never come back again. I was supposed to stay off for four months, but I went back after two by forging my doctor's signature on an insurance release. They set me to mixing mortar and carrying twenty-pound blocks.

I got the knobs and the lock out of the old door and took them back into the house. She was sitting on an ottoman. She had on dark stockings. I told her I'd probably bring another boy

with me the next night, to lay the linoleum. She just nodded.
It was like she was listening to something in her head. I didn't
know what I'd do if my back got to hurting so bad I couldn't
work. I didn't know how bad it would have to hurt before it
stopped me. I didn't know how I'd pay Tracey's doctor bills if
that happened.

I told her I'd take that beer now if she didn't care. She
nodded and smiled and went to get it. I watched her, and I
thought about the twenty dollars she had talked me out of. I
should have just told her to forget it. I should have just told her
to get somebody else and keep her lousy twenty dollars.

He was certainly a fast worker. I didn't know if he wanted
a glass or not. I figured carpenters usually drank theirs straight
out of the can. He wasn't making it easy for me to talk to him.
He acted like he had things on his mind. We couldn't talk at all
with all that ripping and hammering going on.

I carried the beer out to him and he drank about half of it in
one swallow. I sat down again to watch him work and asked him
if he wanted a cigarette. He had some of his own. He picked up
the lock and the knobs and started putting them into the door.

I asked her if she was going to be at home the next night.
I had to ask her twice. She looked up and I told her that I'd
probably get through with the doors that night. I told her that if
she didn't care, I'd go ahead and tear out the old linoleum and
lay the new the next night. If she didn't care.

She'd pulled her dress up over her legs. Her legs were kind of skinny but they weren't that bad. I didn't know if she meant to do it on purpose or not. Maybe she was so drunk she didn't notice it.

She didn't know if she was going to be home the next night or not. She asked me if I wanted to come back the next night. I told her I'd just like to get through. The quicker I got through, the quicker I got paid. She said she'd have to decide.

I knew he wasn't going to be interested in me. The only thing he was interested in was the money. He couldn't wait to get out of my house. And I'd been sitting there thinking such foolish things. I was ashamed of myself. I don't know anything about dating, I've been married so long. Going out to bars alone, hoping for some man to pick me up: I don't want that kind of life. My drink was almost empty.

I told him I needed a fresh one and got up to make it. I didn't know I was in such bad shape. My head started swimming when I got in the kitchen. I dropped my glass.

I heard a glass break and I stopped what I was doing. I got up and looked around. I didn't see her anywhere. Then I heard her. I thought maybe she'd fallen and hurt herself. She sounded like she was crying. I went down the hall and found her in the kitchen. She was down on her knees, on a towel she had folded underneath her. She was crying and picking up the broken pieces of glass. I didn't know what the hell to do.

I know you're not supposed to feel sorry for yourself. But I had always had somebody to take care of me and tell me what to do. It's so frightening to be alone. I was only trying to reach out to somebody. All I wanted was a little conversation. I was just trying to be nice to him.

I was so ashamed for him to see me crying. I'd just had too much to drink and I'd gotten depressed. He was standing behind me. He asked me if I was okay and I said I was. It was so quiet. The glass had gone everywhere. I wanted to make sure I got it all up so I wouldn't step on a tiny piece while I was barefoot one morning. I told him that it was okay, that he could go back to work, that I'd get him another beer in a minute. Then he knelt down beside me and started helping me pick up the glass.

She seemed so helpless and so weak. She wasn't anything like Betty. She wasn't hard like Betty. I know it embarrassed her for me to see her like that. And I was afraid she might cut herself, so I got down on the floor to help her. She was trying to stop crying. I didn't know what was wrong or what to say. I felt bad for her, and I wanted to help her if I could. All her mascara had run down from her eyes in black streaks. She'd smeared some of it wiping at her eyes. She said it was nice of me to help her. Then she said Richard. That was the first time she'd said my name.

I looked at him. He was just as embarrassed as I was. I thought about how I must have looked to him, half drunk, with my eyes red from crying. I had cried so much because of Harold. Nobody knows what I went through. He wasted so much of my life. All those years that were just thrown away. I wanted to tell him so bad about what had happened to me. I had so much on me that I wanted to unload. I turned to him and I put my hand on his shoulder. I wanted him to kiss me, or to put his hand on my breast. Or to at least hold me. I wanted to tell him what was wrong with me.

I didn't know what to say when she touched me. I stopped what I was doing and I looked at her. She was trying to smile. Her eyes were wet. I didn't know what she wanted. Maybe just somebody to listen to her. Maybe something else. But she was old enough to be my mother.

She said what if somebody asked you to do something. And it wouldn't hurt you, if it was just a favor that somebody wanted you to do, would you do it? If it didn't cost you anything and it would help the other person. She said if I just knew. She said he had other women. That he'd beaten her. That nobody knew what she'd been through.

She started crying again. She put her head on my shoulder and she took my hand and slipped it around her waist. I didn't know what else to do but hold her. She started sort of moaning.

I didn't have time to do anything. She said I want you. She put her mouth on mine. She was holding my ears in both her hands. I tried to pull back. I tried to tell her that she was drunk and she didn't know what she was doing. But she unbuckled my pants. It happened in a second. She pulled it out and started rubbing it with her hands, moaning. She leaned back and pulled up her dress and I ran my hands up underneath her. I couldn't help it. I didn't know what to do. I knew she was drunk and I was afraid she'd holler rape when she sobered up. We got up somehow and went back against the counter. She opened her dress and pulled my head down to her. I couldn't get away and didn't want to.

I just went crazy for a minute. Once I touched him I couldn't stop myself. He started running his hands all over me. I knew I should stop but I couldn't. I didn't even know him. I knew he was going to think I was a whore.

I just lost control of myself. I didn't even care what he thought. I just wanted someone to put his arms around me and hold me tight. I didn't want to stop. I knew if we kept on it was going to happen. I wasn't even thinking about how I'd feel the next morning, or how I'd feel after it was over. I was just thinking about how I didn't ever want him to stop. But finally he did. He stopped and backed away from me. He looked like he was scared to death. I don't know what I looked like. Half my clothes were off. I think I asked him what was wrong.

I finally got ahold of myself. I think I said shit or something. We were both breathing hard. I fastened my pants back up. She was staring at me like a wild woman. There was a chair pulled out beside the table and I went over to it and sat down. She didn't say anything for a minute. I think she was buttoning her dress. I waited until I thought she was done and then I turned around and looked at her. She was wiping her eyes with her fingers. She fixed herself another drink. Then she went to the refrigerator and got me another beer. I started to just get up and leave. But she brought the beer and her drink over and set them down and dropped into the chair beside me. She looked dazed. We almost did it, she said. Yeah, I said. We almost did.

He started talking about the little girl. At first I wasn't listening. I was almost in shock. It took a long time for me to calm down. My heart was beating too fast, and I was wet. I wanted to kiss him again but I was scared to try. He said she wasn't his. It was something about her telling him she was divorced and then later after he'd been living with her for a while, admitting that she had never been married. I think I was just staring at my drink when he started talking. But then what he was saying started sinking in and I started listening to him. I couldn't believe what we were doing, just sitting there in my kitchen talking and drinking after what we'd done. He said it didn't matter to him for a while about the lie she had told him because he loved the little girl and felt like she was his. He was the only daddy she'd known. But he didn't love the woman. I could tell that just from hearing him talk. He said he carried the little girl everywhere he went, even if he was just going to the store for something.

There was something wrong with her legs. She couldn't walk right. They had all these tests done on her and had her fitted with braces and then his insurance company wouldn't pay the bills because he wasn't married to her mother. I wondered what she looked like. I had this picture of black hair and a frowning face for some reason. He said he was afraid to leave her. He said he didn't love her, but he couldn't leave the little girl. He said he didn't know what would happen to her. I felt better about everything, about losing my head, after we talked for a while. But he was working all these jobs at night to try and pay the doctor bills. I felt like . . . I just don't know what I felt like. Cheap. Stingy. For getting him to lower his price. And I felt awful for drinking too much and having those daydreams about him, and then kissing him and all. He kept talking. The more he talked, the worse I felt over feeling so sorry for myself about Harold.

I asked him what he was going to do. He said he didn't know. He said if he left her there was no telling what would happen to them. He said the woman had never worked a day in her life and didn't finish high school and had been brought up on welfare. He said she didn't know what it was like to have to work for a living.

I shouldn't have talked so much. I didn't mean to tell her all my problems. I know everybody's got problems, and everybody thinks theirs are worse than everybody else's. I know she had it bad. Married to a son of a bitch that slapped her around. She felt like her whole life had been wasted. She talked some, too. She said she knew what it felt like to have to stay with somebody without love. She knew what I felt like. She was as miserable as I was.

I probably could have taken right back up where we left off. I was tempted to. I don't think I've touched a woman who was that hot ever. I thought when women got older they didn't care anything about sex. Or maybe she was just trying to reach out to somebody. She didn't come right out and say it, but just from the things she said, I could tell she hadn't slept with her ex-husband for years. I felt so goddamn sorry for her. But I didn't want her to feel sorry for me. I didn't want to work anymore, though. I just wanted to load my shit up and go somewhere. I thought about asking her if she wanted to go drink a few beers with me, but really I wanted to be by myself. I had to decide what I was going to do. I knew I couldn't keep going the way I was going.

I asked him what he was going to do and he said he didn't know. He said he'd keep on working. He was hoping she'd grow out of it. He said he didn't mean to dump all his problems on me. But he said the little girl would sit on the floor and hold her arms up to him when he came in from work and beg him to take her. He said he thought she sat on the floor all day because her mother wouldn't help her try to walk or even pick her up. He said all she did was read magazines and watch TV. I don't know how he could have gotten mixed up with somebody like that. I don't know why he couldn't have gotten somebody who deserved him.

I told her that if she didn't care I'd just leave the doors and finish up the next night, or the next. I had to get away. I hated to just leave her wall like that, but there wasn't any way I could finish hanging the door that night. She said it would be okay, that I could come back and finish it whenever I wanted to. She said she never had any company and nobody would see it anyway.

I watched him roll up his cord and put away his tools and get ready to leave. I wanted him to stay, but I didn't ask him to. I could tell he had a lot on his mind. His hands had felt so good to me. I knew I was going to cry after he left. I knew I was going to cry and I knew I was going to drink some more. I wanted him right then more than I've ever wanted anything in my life. I would have given him anything. But all he wanted was to leave. I wasn't going to try to hold him. I wasn't going to make a fool of myself again. But right up until the time he left, I would have made a fool of myself. Gladly. When he went out the door I knew I'd never see him again.

I rode around for a while. I didn't want to go back home just yet. I wanted to run but I didn't have any place to run to. Some people can just walk away, turn their backs and go on and forget about it. I couldn't. But it didn't stop me from thinking about it.

I went to a bar on Jackson Avenue and counted my money before I went inside. There was just enough left from what I'd borrowed from Leon to get a couple of pitchers of draft. There wasn't anybody in there I knew. I sat at a table by myself, in a booth in a dark corner. I thought that if I sat quietly by myself in the dark and drank, I'd be able to figure out what to do with the rest of my life.

Florida was the best place to go. There was no cold weather to stop you from laying brick. There was plenty of building going on. Jobs were supposed to be easy to get.

But I couldn't stop thinking about Myra down on the floor, crying. Or about how she felt when I was kissing her. I'd never had anybody want me that bad. I'd never had anybody so desperate reach out to me like that. And I'd turned her down. I regretted it.

I kept drinking. Betty didn't know what it was like to have to work, to be strapped into a job like a mule in a harness. The company I worked for didn't give a fuck if I broke my back. They'd just hire somebody else. There were people standing in lines all over the country wanting jobs. She didn't understand that. She didn't know what it was like to have to work when you were hurt. You either kept up or you didn't. If you didn't keep up they'd let you go.

She looked so awful down on the floor. I was still thinking about her by the time I finished the first pitcher. I had to scrape all my change together to make the price of the last one. I knew I'd be drunk by the time I finished it, but I didn't care. I wanted to get drunk. I felt like getting drunk would help me more than just about anything right then. So I got the other pitcher and sat back down in the corner with it. I knew by then that it had been wrong for me to turn her down. And I needed to talk to her some more anyway. She had listened to me and she had seemed to understand. She was so much kinder than Betty, so much gentler. Her body had been so soft. I wanted to take all her clothes off gently and touch her whole body and make her happy. I wanted to heal her. I kept drinking. The more I thought about it, the more it seemed like a good idea.

I know I was too drunk to remember what happened exactly. I came to in the parking lot. Somebody had hit me because there was blood in my mouth. I tried to stand. I made it up to my knees and then I passed out.

I woke up again. I was lying beside my truck. I got ahold of the door handle and pulled myself up with that. I leaned my arms on the bed and tried to remember what had happened. Somebody had been yelling at me. I remembered swinging one time. Then nothing until I came to in the parking lot.

I knew what I had to do. I knew where I had to go. I got in my truck and cranked it up. I had to close one eye to see how to drive. Some of my lower teeth were loose. There was a cut inside my mouth. But I knew somebody who would take care of me. I knew somebody who would be glad to see me.

All my crying was over with. You can only cry so much. You can't just keep on feeling sorry for yourself. I was lying in bed watching "The Love Boat" and hoping somehow that he'd come back. But I knew he wouldn't. I didn't know if he'd even come back and finish the work. I thought he would probably be too embarrassed to.

I was watching the show but I didn't believe in it. It wasn't like real life. There were too many happy endings on it. Everybody always found just exactly what they were looking for. And nobody on there was mean. Nobody on there was going to break down a door and slap somebody off the commode.

I wanted to talk to him again. He seemed to be such an understanding person, a person who would take the time to listen to another person's troubles. I was wishing I could see what his woman and his baby looked like. I was still having some drinks.

I knew there were nice men in the world, men who would love me for myself and not mistreat me. But how did you find them? How did you know they wouldn't change years later? There weren't any promises that would keep forever. Things altered in your lives and people changed. Sometimes they even started hating each other. I hated Harold so bad when I divorced him that I couldn't stand to look at him. But I can still remember how tender his hands used to be. I can still remember the first time he undressed me and how he looked at me when I was naked.

But who would want me now? I shouldn't have been surprised when Richard pulled away. I have varicose veins and my breasts are sagging. I've got those ugly rolls of fat around my middle. I've gone through the change. No, a young man doesn't want an old woman. It's the old woman who wants the young man.

I hoped he wouldn't tell anybody. I hoped he wouldn't tell his woman about it. I knew he wouldn't. Not a nice boy like him. I wanted to blame something, so I blamed the drinking. But I couldn't blame all of it on the drinking. I had to blame part of it on me.

I even thought about calling him. But I couldn't call him. What if his woman answered? What would I say then? He might have already told her and she might want to know if this was the old drunk bag who tried to get Richard in the bed with her. She might say, Listen, you old dried up bag of shit. . . .

But what if he answered? It wasn't late. It wasn't even ten o'clock. But what if the baby was asleep and it woke her up? It was stupid to even think about it. But I wanted him to come back so bad. Nobody thinks the things I think. The crazy things, the awful things, the insane things. That's what I was thinking when I heard him pull up.

I don't even know what I said to her. I was almost too drunk to walk. She turned the porch light on and came to the door. I talked to her. I guess I scared her with all the blood I had on me. I know I looked awful. I can't even remember what I said to her. There's no telling what I said to her. It's a wonder she didn't call the police.

I couldn't believe he came back. All that time of lying there thinking about him and wishing he'd come back and then he did. I just had on my housecoat and my underwear. I still had my makeup on. I couldn't wait to let him in.

I turned on the porch light and watched him try to get out of his truck. I didn't know what was wrong with him at first. He was staggering. And his face was all bloody. He'd been in a fight.

I got scared then. It took him about three tries to get up on the porch, and then he had to hold onto a post. He was the drunkest human I'd ever seen. I almost didn't recognize him.

He knocked on the door. I didn't know whether to open it or not. I hadn't been expecting him to be the way he was. I didn't know what to do. He kept knocking and finally I slipped the chain on and opened the door just a crack. I was scared to let him in.

He was weaving. He had blood all over his chin. He could just barely talk. It was hard to understand what he was saying, but he said something about it being so late. I said Yes, it was, and I asked him what he wanted. He said he just wanted to talk to me. I don't know what I could have been thinking of. He looked dangerous.

I told him he was drunk and I asked him again what he wanted. He kept saying that he'd sober up in a little bit. Then he asked me if he could come in. I told him it was awfully late. I didn't even really know him. I didn't know what he might do while he was drunk. He'd already been fighting, what else would he do? I knew that if I let him in he'd never leave, or he'd pass out and I wouldn't know what to do with him. Or what if he tried to rape me? I couldn't let him in.

I tried to be as gentle with him as I could. I told him it would be better if he went on home. I told him it was after ten.

He asked me if I had any coffee. He said if he had some coffee he'd sober up. But he could barely stand. And he was driving. I thought, What if he left in his truck and killed somebody, or himself, before he got home? Maybe I should have let him stay. But I was scared to let him stay. He looked so wild. His eyes were as red as blood.

He said something about a favor. He said something about if it wouldn't hurt you and would help the other person. I didn't know what he was talking about. I told him to please go home.

He said he needed to talk to me, that nobody understood. I told him I didn't want to do anything that would hurt him, but that he needed to go home right away.

I knew I had to be firm. I told him I was going to close the door. He hung his head. Then he looked up and looked into my eyes. Looked right into me. Everything changed in that moment. I saw how the rest of my life was going to be. I knew that I would always be lonely, and that I would always be scared. I told him to go home again and then I shut the door.

I don't remember driving home. I just woke up the next morning in bed with Betty. Tracey was crying. It was dark. I put my hand on Betty and I moved against her and I put my chin in her neck. She squeezed my hand in her sleep. She moved it down between her legs and moaned. Maybe she was having a bad dream. It all came back to me suddenly, what I'd done the night before. I just closed my eyes. I didn't want to think about it. I had to get up in thirty more minutes. I had to get up and fix myself some breakfast.

Some men showed up a few days later. One of them was short, with a red beard. His shirt was spattered with paint. He did all the talking. The other one just stood on the porch and looked around.

I let them in after they explained why they were there. They brought their tools in, and the linoleum in. I stayed in the bedroom while they hammered and sawed and nailed. I thought they never would get through.

Finally he knocked on the door and asked me if I wanted to come out and look at it. I went out and looked. The doors were hung and the new linoleum was down. They'd done a neat job, a good job. But I wanted them out of my house. I wrote him a check quickly, for the same price that Richard had named. They took his sawhorses. They said they could do other things: remodeling, build decks, paint my house. I thanked them and told them I didn't need anything else right now. I didn't ask them anything about Richard.

It was almost a month later when I saw them in the supermarket. I like to do my shopping at night, when the stores aren't full of people, when the aisles are clear and you can take your time. A young woman turned into the aisle ahead of me, a girl with a sweatshirt and blue jeans and fuzzy blue house shoes. I wouldn't be caught dead out like that. There was a little girl with yellow hair sitting in the cart, and she was reaching out for everything they passed. The woman slapped at the child's hands like an automatic reaction, without even looking.

I watched them for a while. And then I went on past them. I wanted to finish and get out of the store quickly, as soon as possible, before it was too late. Their lives were things that didn't concern me and the world is full of suffering anyway. How can one person be expected to do anything about it?

I turned the corner and he was standing at the meat counter with a pack of bacon in his hand. His back was turned and I thought I might slip by. But he turned his head, just a little, and he saw me. He didn't seem surprised, or even embarrassed. His head bent just a little, and he said something. Hey, something. I thought for a moment he was going to start talking to me. But he didn't. He turned away. I thought that was nice of him, to make it so easy for me to go on by. I didn't let myself hurry. I stopped a little ways past him and looked at some dill pickles in a display set up in the middle of the floor. There were hundreds of bottles. I didn't want to buy any, but I picked up one and read the price. It was fifty-nine cents. I looked over my shoulder and he was looking at me. Richard. My hand must have been trembling. I wanted him even then. I set the jar back without looking and the whole display crashed down. I jumped back. It was unbelievable the way it looked. Broken glass everywhere, and thousands of tiny green chips. Green juice that started puddling around my cart. It ran across the floor and people stepped out of the aisles to look at me. I was trying to think of something to say. I didn't look over my shoulder to see if Richard was watching. I was scared of what I might see.

I put the groceries away and took a shower and put on clean clothes. Tracey was asleep in her bed and Betty was asleep in hers. I waited until she started snoring and then I started gathering things up. I had a week's pay in my pocket and the truck was paid for. I had the title in the glove box. I could trade it off, buy another one, whatever.

Tracey doesn't sleep well most nights, but that night she did. She slept through Grenada, through Jackson, on through Hattiesburg. The miles piled up behind us. I knew Betty wouldn't send anybody after us. I knew Betty would probably be relieved.

I had Myra's number in my pocket and I thought I might call her when we got to where we were going. I thought I might wish her some luck.

THE END OF ROMANCE

Miss Sheila and I were riding around, as we often did in those days. But I was pretty sure it was going to be the last afternoon of our relationship. Things hadn't been good lately.

It was hot. We'd been drinking all day, and we'd drunk almost enough. We lacked just a little getting to a certain point. I'd already come to a point. I'd come down to the point where I could still get an erection over her, but my heart wouldn't be going crazy and jumping up in my throat like a snake-bit frog. I wouldn't be fearing for my life when I mounted her. I knew it was time for me to book for a fat man's ass. She bitched about how much time I spent locked in my room, how my mother was bossy, when would I ever learn some couth? And you get them started nagging at you, you might as well be married. Well. I'd been out of women when I found her and I'd be out of women again until I found another one. But there were hundreds of other women, thousands, millions. They'd been making new ones every day for years.

"I ain't drunk," she said.

"Well, I'm not drunk, either."

"You look like you are."

"So do you."

"You got enough money to get some more? You can take all that Nobel Prize money and get us a coupla sixers, can't you?"

She was bad about chagrinning me like that.

"I magine I can manage it," I said.

So she whipped it into one of those little quick-joints that are so popular around here, one of those chicken-scarfing places, whipped it up in front of the door and stopped. She stared straight ahead through the windshield. Nothing worse than a drunken woman. Empty beer cans were all piled up around our feet. The end of romance is never easy.

"What matter?" I said.

"Nuttin matter. Everything just hunkin funkin dunky."

"You mean hunky dory?"

She had some bloodshot eyes and a ninety-yard stare. I'd known it would come down to this. The beginning of romance is wonderful. I don't know why I do it over and over. Starting with a new one, I can just about eat her damn legs off. Then, later, some shit like this. Women. Spend your whole life after the right one and what do they do? Shit on you. I always heard the theory of slapping them around to make them respect you, that that's what they want. But I couldn't. I couldn't stand to hit that opposite flesh. That slap would ring in my head for the rest of my life. This is what I do: take what they give and give what I can and when it's over find another one. Another one. That's what's so wonderful about the beginning of romance. She's different. She's new. Unique. Everything's fresh. Crappola. You go in there to shave after the first night and what does she do while you've got lather all over your face? Comes in and hikes her nightgown and then the honeymoon's over.

I'm not trying to get away from the story. I mean, just a few minutes later, some stuff actually happened. But sitting in that car at that moment, I was a little bitter. I had all sorts of thoughts going through my head, like: *Slapper. Slapper ass off.* I held that down.

She looked at me with those bloodshot eyes. "You really somethin, you know that? You really really really."

I knew it was coming. We'd had a bad afternoon out at the lake. Her old boyfriend had been out there, and he'd tried to put the make on her. I and seven of my friends had ripped his swim trunks off of him, lashed him to the front of her car, and driven him around blindfolded but with his name written on a large piece of beer carton taped to his chest for thirty-seven minutes, in front of domestic couples, moms and dads, family reunions, and church groups. She hadn't thought it was funny. We, we laughed our asses off.

I got out of the car. She didn't want to have any fun, that was fine with me. I bent over and gathered up an armload of beer cans and carried them to the trash can. They clattered all over the place when I dropped them in. I was a little woozy but I didn't think anybody could see it. Through the window

of the store this old dyed woman with great big breasts and
pink sunglasses looked out at me with a disapproving frown. I
waved. Then I went back for more cans.

"Don't worry about the damn cans, all right?"

"I can't move my feet for them," I said.

"I'll worry about the damn cans," she said.

It sort of crumpled me. We were in her convertible, and
once it was fun to just throw them straight up while we were
going down the road. The wind, or I guess just running out
from under them was fun. It was a game. Now it didn't seem to
matter. I think we both had the creep of something bad coming
up on us. She could have beat the shit out of me, I could have
beat the shit out of her. It's no way to live. You don't want to
go to sleep nervous, fearing the butcher knife, the revolver, the
garrote.

"Just go in and get some beer," she said. "We got to talk."

Then she started crying. She wasn't pretty when she was
crying. Her whole face turned red and wrinkled up. I knew it
was me. It's always me.

"You're just so damn great, ain't you?" she said. "Don't
even want nobody overt the house, cept a bunch of old drunks
and freaks and whores."

My friends. Poets, artists, actors, English professors out at
Ole Miss. She called them drunks and freaks. *Slapper. Slap shit
out of her.*

"Just go on git the damn beer," she said. "I got something
to tell you."

It's awful to find pussy so good that treats you so bad. It's like you've got to *pay* for it being good. But you've got to be either a man or a pussy. You can't just lay around and pine. I thought at that point that maybe I'd gotten out of that particular car for the last time.

I went on in. I was even starting to feel better. If she left, I could go home, open all the doors, crank up the stereo, get free. I could start sleeping in the daytime and writing at night again, nonstop if I wanted to, for eight or ten hours. I could have a party without somebody sullen in one corner. Everything would be different and the same again.

Well, hell, I wasn't perfect though, was I? I'd probably been a shitass a few times. Who's not? Even your best friend will turn asshole on you from time to time. He's only human.

I knew somebody else would come along. I just didn't know how long it would be. So I did a little quick rationalizing inside the store.

Whatever I was going back outside to wasn't going to be good. She was bracing herself up to be nasty to me, I could see that. And there wasn't any need in a bit of it. I could do without all the nastiness. I could take an amicable breakup. All I had to do was hang around inside the store for a while, and she'd probably get tired of waiting for me, and run off and leave me. So I went back toward the rear. The old bag was watching me. She probably thought I was a criminal. All I was doing was sitting back there gnawing my fingernails. But it was no good. I couldn't stand to know she was out there waiting on me.

So I got back up and went up the beer aisle. I figured I might as well go on and face it. Maybe we'd have a goodbye roll. I got her a sixpack of Schlitz malt liquor and got myself a sixer of Stroh's in bottles. The old bag was eyeing me with distaste. I still had my trunks on, and flip-flops, and my FireBusters T-shirt. I was red from passing out under the sun.

I could see Miss Sheila out there. I set the beer on the counter just as a black guy pulled up beside her car and got out. I started pulling my money out and another car pulled up beside the first one. It had a black guy in it, too, only this one had a shotgun. The first black guy was up against the door, just coming in, and the second black guy suddenly blew the top of the first black guy's head off. The first black guy flopped inside.

"*AAAAAAAAAAAHHHHHHHHHHHH!*" he said. "*HHHH-HHWWWWWWWWAAAAAAAAAAAAAAAAHHH!*" Blood and meat and black hair had flown inside everywhere with him, glass. It stuck to the walls, to the cigarettes in the rack over the counter, to the warming oven where they had the fried chicken. I'd eaten a lot of that fried chicken. The guy flopped down the detergent aisle. "*WAAAAAAAAAAAAAAAH!*" he said.

I just stood there holding my money. I'd been wrong. The top of his head hadn't been blown off after all. He just didn't have any hair up there.

"*HAAAAAAAAAAAAAAAAAAH!*" he said. He was flopping around like a fish. He flopped down to the end of the aisle, then flopped over a couple of tables where people ate their barbecue at lunchtime, (where I'd been sitting just a few minutes before) and then he flopped over in the floor. I looked outside. The second black guy had gotten back into his car with his shotgun and was backing out of the parking lot. I couldn't see Miss Sheila.

"Let me pay for my beer and get out of here," I said, to the woman who had ducked down behind the counter. "The cops'll be here in a minute."

The black guy got off the floor back there and flopped over the meat market. "*AAAAAAAAAAAAAH!*" he said. He flopped up against the coolers, leaving big bloody handprints all over the glass. He started flopping up the beer aisle, coming back toward us.

"Come on, lady," I said. "Shitfire."

He flopped over a bunch of Vienna sausage and Moon Pies, and then he flopped over the crackers and cookies. Blood was pouring out of his head. I looked down at one of the coolers and saw a big piece of black wool sliding down the glass in some blood. He was tracking it all over the store, getting it everywhere.

I knew what the beer cost. It was about six dollars. I didn't wait for a sack. But I watched him for a moment longer. I couldn't take my eyes off him. He flopped over the candy and the little bags of potato chips, and across the front, and flopped across the chicken warmer and the ice cream box and the magazine racks. "*HAAAAAAAAAAAAH!*" he said. I put some money up on the counter. Then I went outside.

The guy had shot the whole place up. All the glass in the windows was shattered, and he'd even shot the bricks. He'd even shot the newspaper machines. He'd murdered the hell out of *The Oxford Eagle*.

When I looked back inside, the guy had flopped up against the counter where the woman was hiding, flopping all over the cash register. Sheila wasn't dead or murdered either one.

I asked her, "You all right?" She was down in the floorboard. She looked up at me. She didn't look good.

"I thought you's dead," she screamed. "*OH, GOD, HOW COULD I HAVE BEEN SO FOOLISH?*"

I set the beer on the back seat and got in. "You better git this sumbitch outa here," I said. I reached over and got me a beer. I could hear the sirens coming. They were wailing way off in the distance. She latched onto me.

"*I WOULDN'T LEAVE YOU NOW FOR NOTHIN,*" she screamed. "*COULDN'T RUN ME OFF,*" she hollered.

"I'm telling you we better get our ass out of here," I said.

"Look out," she screamed. I looked. The wounded black guy was flopping through the door where there wasn't any door anymore. He flopped up beside the car. "*WAAAAAAAAAAH!*" he said. He was slinging blood all over us. But other than that he seemed harmless.

"What I wanted to say was maybe we should watch more TV together," she said. "If you just didn't write so much. . . ."

The cops screamed into the parking lot. They had their shotguns poking out the windows before they even stopped. Five or six cruisers. Blue uniforms and neat ties and shiny brass. They'd taken their hats off. They had shiny sunglasses. You could tell that they were itching to shoot somebody, now that they'd locked and loaded. The black guy was leaning against the car, heaving. I knew I wouldn't get to finish my beer. I heard them shuck their pumps. I raised my hands and my beer. I pointed to Miss Sheila.

"She did it," I said.

THE BRIGHT LEAF SHORT FICTION SERIES